Showdown on Texas Flat

Showdown on Texas Flat

RAY HOGAN

THORNDIKE
CHIVERS

This Large Print edition is published by Thorndike Press®, Waterville, Maine USA and by BBC Audiobooks, Ltd, Bath, England.

Published in 2004 in the U.S. by arrangement with Golden West Literary Agency.

Published in 2004 in the U.K. by arrangement with Golden West Literary Agency.

U.S. Hardcover 0-7862-6215-X (Western)
U.K. Hardcover 0-7540-9945-8 (Chivers Large Print)
U.K. Softcover 0-7540-9946-6 (Camden Large Print)

The text of this Large Print edition is unabridged.
Other aspects of the book may vary from the original edition.

Set in 16 pt. Plantin by Minnie B. Raven.

Printed in the United States on permanent paper.

British Library Cataloguing-in-Publication Data available

Library of Congress Cataloging-in-Publication Data

Hogan, Ray, 1908–
    Showdown on Texas Flat / Ray Hogan.
      p. cm.
    ISBN 0-7862-6215-X (lg. print : hc : alk. paper)
    1. Ranch life — Fiction.   2. Large type books.   I. Title.
PS3558.O3473S53 2004
813'.54—dc22   2003067196

Showdown
on Texas Flat

1

Grim, Dave Bradford stood in the shade fronting his low-roofed ranchhouse and waited. Farman and his two gunnies were just turning into his yard, passing under the high crosspiece of the gate a quarter mile distant.

A taut, knowing smile pulled at his lips. Wherever JJ went so also went Macklin and Casey. They were as shadows to the big rancher, still-faced, quiet spoken men who had become known in the Cebolla Basin as Farman's enforcers.

Now they were paying a call on him . . . The coolness that had seen Bradford through a half a hundred similar crises during that period of his life when he had hired out as a deputy marshal, a shotgun rider, bullion guard and the like, now settled though him, tightening the corners of his jaw, narrowing his deep-set gray eyes. He'd hoped to avoid trouble with JJ Farman but it wasn't to be.

He stirred, shrugged. It never was where the JJ Farmans were concerned, he thought, and glanced at the silent men gathered nearby. The Farmans always had to have their way and they set out to get it by any means at their command.

His attention paused on the broad face of Stan Auerbach whose place was some miles to the south. Stan was a big-bodied man with a temper to match. He hoped the young rancher would be able to keep himself in hand when Farman began laying down the law to them. The cattleman wasn't accustomed to being crossed, and Stan, losing his head and spouting off, could find himself in bad trouble.

He had been in a bad mood when he arrived, and this waiting around for Farman had not improved things any. Like all the others present — Nate Wheeler, Pete Drury, Clem Gillis, Calvin Yates, and old José Rodriguez, who had a small combination farm and ranch at the extreme lower end of the Basin, he had been summoned by rider to be in attendance at Bradford's at five o'clock sharp for a meeting. Being so ordered had rubbed him the wrong way.

Auerbach was not alone in his irritation. Farman's peremptory command had the same effect upon them all — but they had

8

come, nevertheless, some hiding their sullen anger, others making no bones about showing it. To most, JJ Farman was not a man to trifle with and one who, when he hollered *frog*, expected everyone within hearing distance to say, *how far?*

But the rancher, if his purpose was for that which Dave suspected, was in for a surprise insofar as he was concerned. He'd always managed to get along with the cattle-man whose hundred thousand acre spread lay to the northeast of his own moderately sized outfit, but he reckoned that was so simply because there had never been any cause for conflict.

Bradford had given up wearing a gun for gain some seven years previous, after finally accumulating the stake he'd worked for, and settling in the Basin, had become involved in realizing the dream of his life — that of building for himself a good cattle ranch with a side-line of raising horses especially suited and trained for working beef.

Matters had gone well for him. He'd gotten the breaks; he now had better than six hundred head of prime beef wearing his Spur brand while his herd of horses numbered upwards of fifty. He had a good, tight, if somewhat basic ranchhouse, all the necessary outbuildings including quarters for twice the number of hired hands he presently employed — an even half a dozen including old Milt Fresno, the cook — and now he was ready to start spreading out and growing in earnest.

For one thing, it was necessary; he needed more good breeding stock, additional equipment, a larger barn, a feed storage building, and he wanted to enlarge and improve the main house in preparation for the day — soon, he hoped — when he would feel it was right to ask Pete Drury's daughter, Sirral, to become his wife.

It would all take money, and to get it he had decided to sell off four hundred beeves. The six thousand dollars, more or less, that he'd get for them at Wichita, would accomplish all the things he had planned and furnish him with a cash surplus as well.

All the other ranchers in the Basin, just getting themselves on firm footing, were in the same wagon, and when he had dropped the word that he was trailing a herd to the railhead that spring, each had decided he, too, should convert a portion of their stock into badly needed hard money.

Nate Wheeler, whose ranch adjoined

10

Dave's to the immediate south, felt the need to sell a hundred head — half of his total herd. Pete Drury was parting with only twenty-five, while Clem Gillis and aged José Rodriguez cut out only ten steers each. Yates turned up with twenty, leaving Stan Auerbach to top all but Bradford with a hundred and fifty head.

All combined, Dave had a total of over seven hundred steers destined for Wichita — a small herd as cattle drives went, but each beef represented much hard work and sacrifice for every man involved and thereby counted doubly in importance.

Since none of the ranchers and homesteaders had crews large enough or wished to part with sufficient steers to make a drive profitable, they had called on Dave when the fact became known that he was trailing a herd, and asked that he permit them to throw their cattle in with his. They would pro-rate and share losses, they said, and would pay him a ten percent commission on their respective receipts for the favor.

Bradford had given the request an overnight's consideration. He had the necessary crew, all with drover's experience, and the additional cattle would make little difference. He agreed to accept the responsi-

bility, refusing the commission offer, however and agreeing only to the pro-rating of
losses which he felt could be kept to a minimum.

In turn Wheeler and Pete Drury would
look after his place during the month or so
that he would be away, helping out the two
elderly punchers he planned to leave behind. It should work out well for everyone
concerned; he would be able to make the
drive, convert the herd into money needed
by all of them, while Spur would not go
neglected . . . At least, that was the way it
had worked out in his mind.

"About time he was showing up." Stan
Auerbach's grumbling voice drew Dave
from his deep thoughts. "Goddammit, he
figures we're like him — got nothing to do
but set around on our tails and watch the
hired help work."

"What hired help?" Gillis muttered.
"Ain't nobody on my place but me and the
old woman and the kids —"

Auerbach threw an angry glance at the
lean, graying oldster in his faded, patched
overalls. "What I'm bitching about! We ain't
got hired hands like him. I get home there'll
still be chores to do — and it'll be dark."

"Same here," Pete Drury added. "Was
half a mind not to come — him sending

that stablehand and ordering me to be here, like he did."

"But I see you come just the same," Wheeler commented drily. "Might as well face up to it — all of us — we're like a bunch of sheep where Farman's concerned. He runs the Basin and we do whut he says."

"He ain't never said nothing to me before," Gillis countered, frowning. "Can't figure what's got into him now. Always just sort of acted like none of us was even alive. You reckon something's happened — something somebody's gone and done that's riled him?"

"He's riled, ain't no doubt of that," Yates said. "Else he'd not have that pair of gunslingers with him."

"That's what he hired them to do — side him when he's cooking up something," Wheeler murmured. "Price a man has to pay when he climbs up and gets to be the biggest duck on the pond . . . Always somebody looking to get even."

Gillis wagged his head. "Maybe so, but I sure ain't ever crossed him . . . Dave, you say you ain't got no idea what this's all about?"

Bradford, arms folded across his chest, shoulders against one of the uprights supporting the roof of the gallery spanning his house, shrugged.

"Figure I do, but it'd be only a guess. Best thing's wait, let him spit it out. Then we'll all know for certain."

"But you got a hunch, I take it."

Dave, cool gaze on JJ Farman and the two men with him, now pulling onto the hard-pack, nodded.

"Knowing his kind, expect so."

"Then, what the hell is it? What's wrong?"

"He'll tell you," Bradford said, coming away from the support and moving slowly into the center of the yard. "Be my guess that it's got something to do with Texas Flat."

2

JJ Farman, in gray corded pants, elaborately decorated and hand-tooled boots, and white silk shirt open at the collar in deference to the afternoon's heat, was an impressive figure. He sat ramrod straight on the blaze-faced bay he rode, knees stiff, broad-brimmed hat pulled low to shade his granite-hard blue eyes.

In direct contrast the two who flanked him were slouched in their saddles, shoulders forward, arms limp, one hand grasping the reins of their mounts, the other hovering close to the pistol thonged to a leg. Casey's thin lips were pulled back into a half smile; Guy Macklin's mouth was a fixed line, his dark features in shadow.

"What's on your mind, Farman?"

Dave Bradford had long ago learned the advantage of taking the initiative regardless of the situation. It worked the same with gun or words.

Anger stirred the rancher. He anchored his gaze on Bradford. "I'll do the talking — you listen," he said coldly.

"Go ahead," Dave replied, equally cool. "Get done with it — then get off my land."

Kurt Casey drew himself up slowly, muttered something at low breath. Farman merely stared. In the sudden tenseness Stan Auerbach, his bravado now replaced by an attitude of servility, moved forward a step.

"We're listening, Mr. Farman," he said in a tone that implied apology for Bradford's rashness.

Casey relaxed gently. The rancher bobbed his head. "I'll make it short and sweet. Word's come to me that you're trailing a herd to Wichita. That true?"

"Well — yes," Auerbach answered, frowning. "We figured — that is, Bradford here figured —"

"I don't give a goddam who figured what! I'm giving you notice that Texas Flat is closed. I don't want you driving cattle across it."

Auerbach nodded hastily. "Whatever you say —"

"He's not speaking for me," Bradford drawled quietly. "Maybe not for some others, either."

16

JJ Farman's brows lifted. "No?"

"No . . . Texas Flat is open range. I'll trail cattle across it any time I've got the need."

"Wrong. That Flat's my range. I aim to keep you or anybody else off it."

Bradford, a rigid, high-shouldered shape in the afternoon sunlight, shook his head. He knew he was baiting the rancher but there was no other way to handle it.

"You're wasting your breath. It's not yours. It's not anybody's."

"I'm running cattle on it — that makes it mine."

"The hell it does," Dave said flatly. "You've no more right to it than any other man."

"The right's mine if I'm big enough to take it and hold it."

"Which is the only grounds you can claim it on. I don't want trouble with you, Farman. Like to keep peace in this country if it can be done, but I don't aim fall down and play dead just because you say so."

JJ Farman studied Dave for a long minute. Finally he shrugged. "Can see now I made my mistake at the start. Should've kept you all out, never let you settle and put up your little two-bit, starve-out spreads. Should have —"

17

"If you'd tried then you'd had trouble right at the beginning. Been all the same."

"Maybe so, but it ain't here nor there. I'm not making another mistake. You want to drive beef to Wichita, you go around the Flat, not across it."

"Not about to," Bradford said softly. "It's two hundred miles farther that way — take an extra ten or twelve days. It's rough country and there's damn little water." He paused, added in a more conciliatory tone, "You're a cattleman. You know well as I do what that would do to cattle."

"I know, but it ain't no worry of mine," Farman said indifferently. "Point I'm making is — you're not taking a herd across my range."

"And I'm telling you again — it's not your range. It's open to everybody. Even so, crossing it wouldn't hurt you any. There'll only be around seven hundred head and they'll be moving all the time. The grass they'll eat won't be missed."

"Not denying that. Point is, I let you jaspers use it, then first thing I know somebody else will be tracking across it. Then next thing there'll be some jaybird squatting on it, trying to start hisself a ranch, or breaking the ground with a damned plow and turning it into dust . . . No, like I said,

I ain't making another mistake."

"And you'll be making a bigger mistake if you don't listen," Kurt Casey said, his flat eyes on Bradford. "Your last one."

Dave swung his attention to the man . . . A cheap gunman, the dime-a-dozen kind. He'd encountered plenty of them during his time in the towns and on the trails, and he buried a few.

"You've got a big mouth, friend," he said coldly. "My advice to you is keep it buttoned and let your boss do the talking."

Casey spurred forward impulsively, hand sweeping down for the gun on his hip. Bradford, unarmed, did not stir. In the same instant the front screen door of the house swung open, banged against the wall. A bearded and graying old man with a cook's apron tucked back out of the way, a double-barreled shotgun in his gnarled hands and leveled at Casey, stepped into full view.

"Whoa-up!" he called sharply. "That is, unless'n you want to get yourself blasted in two by a charge of buckshot."

Kurt Casey froze. Farman watched in silence while Guy Macklin remained motionless on his saddle.

"Maybe you ain't noticed, but Dave ain't wearing no iron . . . Or maybe you did," the old man said pointedly.

Casey, mouth set, backed his horse into place alongside Farman. Without turning Bradford said: "It's all right, Milt."

The cook eased off, fell back a few steps until his shoulders were against the wall. "Maybe so," he said reluctantly, not lowering the shotgun, "but I reckon I'd best keep standing here."

A sigh of relief slipped from the lips of one of the nearby ranchers. Auerbach, visibly shaken, rubbed his palms together nervously.

"There oughtn't to be no need for this," he said, shaking his head. "We're all reasonable men. Seems we could talk this out —"

"Talking's done," Farman cut in harshly. "I've warned you to keep off Texas Flat — and I damned sure mean it."

"And I'm telling you that you don't have that right," Bradford replied stubbornly.

"Got the means, and that's the right, far as I'm concerned."

"But it's not fair to us," Nate Wheeler said, speaking up for the first time. All but Bradford and Auerbach, and the old cook, seemed to have been struck dumb by the appearance of Farman and his gunmen. "Driving a small herd like we're figuring on won't hurt you any, even if you are using the Flat as range."

"And it sure means aplenty to us — not having to circle the Flat and go through the brakes," Pete Drury, emboldened by Wheeler, added.

"Man stands to lose plenty of stock taking that old trail — not counting the wearing down of what he gets through," Wheeler continued.

"No sweat off my hide," Farman said with a wave of his hand. "If you ain't big enough to stand losses, you ain't big enough to be in the cattle business."

Dave Bradford listened to the words being passed back and forth. He had planned to take the herd of combined brands across the broad expanse known as Texas Flat simply because it was days shorter as well as being an easier route that would enable the steers to stand the long trek to the railhead far better.

He had been aware of Farman's claim to the Flat, one based simply on usage and had intended to pay the rancher a call, advise him of his plans to make the passage. But word had leaked out, beat him to it. Now it was a matter of ultimatums — and one of principle. If they bowed to JJ Farman's dictum now, all the ranchers in the

Cebolla Basin would never get off their knees again. He would call the shots and keep them under his thumb for the rest of time.

He glanced about at Wheeler, at Pete Drury, at José Rodriguez and the others wondering how far he could expect them to go in standing with him. Would they back him all the way, or would they, like Stan Auerbach, quail under the threat of violence promised by Farman?

They were all small outfits with Auerbach being the only one coming anywhere near to having a spread as large as his own Spur — which in turn fell far short, of course, of being as large as Farman's J-Bar-J. In reality Rodriguez, Yates, and Clem Gillis were farmers with only a side interest in cattle growing. Could he expect them to side him if it came down to a virtual war with Farman?

He doubted it even though he admitted to himself that such a conflict was as important to them as it would be to him and the others for the history of such men as JJ Farman indicated that once victor in a test of power, they knew no bounds in the future. Gillis, Rodriquez, Yates, and all the rest, would be at the rancher's whim and mercy, and if he ever took a fancy to their land, all of which butted cozily against the foot of Shadow Mountain with the cold, clear water of the Rio Cruzado coursing across the center of each piece of property, he would not hesitate to drive them off and take over.

The time to halt the spread of a poisonous weed was at its first appearance — at the moment when it thrust its first stalk above ground; the same rule applied to the JJ Farmans of the world.

"You agree to that, Dave?"

It was Stan Auerbach's voice that broke into his thoughts. Bradford turned to him, shook his head.

"Reckon I wasn't listening."

Auerbach cleared his throat impatiently. "Was telling Mr. Farman we'd think it over, that maybe it'd be smart to take a bit more time and trail the herd around Texas Flat. We don't want no trouble —"

Dave Bradford ceased listening to the man, faced Farman. He was taking a long step, one that could put him in the open all alone if what he did failed to meet with favor among the other ranchers. But it didn't matter; they could pull out their part of the herd if they so wished; he would make the drive across Texas Flat even if it involved only his own beef. It was

23

that or knuckle under to JJ Farman and he reckoned he was too old at twenty-eight to start doing that for any man.

"All right, you've had your say. Far as I'm concerned you've done nothing but waste my time . . . Get out!"

Farman's color reddened. His jaw clicked shut and as Kurt Casey stiffened, he thrust out a restraining hand, checked the gunman.

"Suit yourself," he murmured, "but don't ever let it be said I never warned you — all of you — fair and square."

"Got me a little warning of my own, too, mister," Guy Macklin added in his quiet way. "Start wearing your gun. Recollect hearing somewheres that you was once some kind of a hell-bender with it. Next time we meet I aim to find out if it's the truth."

Dave Bradford smiled humorlessly. "Be glad to accommodate you — any time," he said and watched the three men wheel and head out across the yard.

3

Wheeler swore softly into the warm hush. Milt Fresno muttered something, turned and entered the house. Auerbach settled his shocked eyes on Dave.

"All hell's to pay now! You shouldn't have ragged him the way you did."

Bradford's reply was dry. "Why not? What gives him the right to say whether we breathe or choke?"

"Not that," Auerbach said, looking down. "I just figure we're fools to look for trouble."

Dave considered the rancher quietly. Then, "You sort of changed your tune, Stan, since you rode in . . . And far as trouble goes, you've got it from now on if you give in to him. His kind never lets up once they know they can push a man around."

"Maybe not —"

"There's no maybe to it! I've been down this road before."

"But you ain't dead sure about him," Auerbach persisted stubbornly. "He's let us be up to now, I think he will again if we don't rub him wrong. And you've got to admit Texas Flat sort of belongs to him. He's been running stock on it for quite a spell."

Bradford hung his thumbs in his waistband, smiled coldly. "You think that gives him the right to keep everybody off it even though it's open range?"

Stan Auerbach nodded slowly. "In a way. He was on it first and that sort of makes it his."

"Not to my way of thinking!" Bradford snapped, and shifted his attention to the others. "You all best make up your mind where you stand. You've got a choice; either you back down, like Auerbach, or you go ahead with our plans. Nothing's changed far as I'm concerned."

Pete Drury paused in the filling of his scorched briar pipe with tobacco shreds. "Meaning you're making the drive across Texas Flat — and to hell with Farman?"

Bradford bucked his head. "For one thing — I'm not about to take my herd two hundred miles out of the way to suit him or anybody else. Besides the waste of time, it would mean walking that much more tallow off every steer I'm selling, not to mention doubling the losses I'll have to take by going through the brakes."

"Better to get there with part of what you started out with than none at all," Auerbach said.

"Might be true in some cases, but not here. There's more to it than that. We let Farman tell us what we can do this time and we'll be squirming under his heel for the rest of our lives. Even if I got through with only ten steers, I'd figure I was ahead in the long run because I would have proved to Farman that he wasn't telling me what I could or couldn't do."

Calvin Yates nodded vigorously. "I'm agreeing with that."

Auerbach threw a hot glance at the older man. "Sure — you can say that! You ain't risking much — twenty stinking steers and that jack-leg outfit of yours —"

Yates cocked his head to one side, spat. "No, reckon not but I expect them twenty steers counts for as much to me as your hundred and fifty does to you. Same goes for my ranch. It ain't much but it's all I got to show for forty years of living and it sure is just as important to me as your place is to you."

The screen door banged again. Milt

Fresno appeared, a clutch of tin cups in one hand, a pot of coffee in the other. Moving through the group, he parceled out the containers to each and then filled them all with steaming black liquid. The task completed, he faced Dave.

"We still making the drive?"

"Nothing's changed," Bradford answered.

"Good. I'll finish getting things ready." He hesitated again. "You want me to figure on a couple extra weeks?"

Dave shook his head. "Nothing's changed," he said again.

Fresno grinned in a pleased way and turned back into the house. Stan Auerbach sloshed the contents of his cup about slowly.

"You're making a mistake, Dave . . . A big one."

Bradford's shoulders stirred. "If it is, I want it to be mine. I think we all ought to stand together in this against Farman, but I won't push any of you to do it. You can pull your beef out of the herd and there'll be no hard feelings."

"I ain't changed my mind none," Yates said at once. "Like you're saying — it's the principle of the thing more'n the cattle."

Auerbach slid a glance at the man. "You

figure you can afford principles?" he asked in a derisive tone.

"If I can't," the rancher said, "then I reckon I've growed this old for nothing."

José Rodriguez, squatting on his haunches, back against the edge of the porch, nodded solemnly. "It is true. A man must be a man. And this Farman. There is a story among my people that is of his kind – the legend of the prairie dog and the small owl that lives in the desert also. The little dog digs the hole for a home but soon the owl comes to visit. In not a long time the owl claims the home and the dog is crowded from it.

"Such is the way here . . . I shall leave my cattle with you, señor. If all are lost I will not grieve for I will have done my part to prevent injustice."

Nate Wheeler, quiet through most of the meeting, abruptly tossed off his coffee, set the cup down on the floor of the porch.

"Goes for me, too, Dave. I'm with you all the way."

Bradford felt the sense of aloneness that had possessed him slipping away. It had appeared to be shaping up into a solitary conflict between Farman and himself, but he had been wrong. First Yates, then Rodriguez and now Nate Wheeler, who would be risking a hundred and fifty steers, an amount second only in number to his own herd, had declared themselves. He wanted them all to be certain, however; they must understand the risk they would be taking.

"Fine," he said, "only I won't have any of you lining up with me unless you realize what could happen. I could lose every cow I start out with."

"I ain't so sure of that," Gillis said, rubbing at the stubble on his chin. "I got a hunch Farman will pull in his horns when he sees we're going ahead with the drive. I'm wondering maybe if he ain't all talk."

"Could be, but to his way of thinking, he's got plenty to lose if we buck him."

"For sure," Wheeler said. "And he's got Casey and Guy Macklin hired on special to keep it from happening."

"Well, I don't figure he's bluffing," Drury added. "He don't have to."

"That's the way I have to look at it," Dave said. "I'd like to think he'll back down when he finds out we didn't scare off, but we'd be fools to plan on it."

"All the same to me," Wheeler said. "I finally got it into my head what the real issue in this thing was and what you were driving at. I say we best stop Farman now or plan on someday getting run clean out of the Basin — and I'm saying this most to you, Stan."

Auerbach only shrugged, stared off across the plain.

Wheeler shook his head, turned again to Dave. "You want any of my hired help or you still figure you'd rather make the drive with your own crew?"

"Obliged but I'll stay with my boys. I'm taking Sam Zu and Jackson — they've both had plenty of drover experience. Then there'll be Ruskin and Rufe Miller. Milt Fresno's driving the chuck wagon and minding the cooking and the remuda."

"About as good a crew as a man could ask for. Strips your place pretty clean but like I told you, don't worry about it. We'll see that it's looked after — Drury and me."

"Appreciate that," Bradford said and glanced to the west, gauged the lowering sun. "Like to get this all settled. Plans are to move out tomorrow right after noon."

"Count me in," Drury said again.

Rodriguez nodded, puffing slowly on his thin Mexican cigarette.

"I ain't changed none," Clem Gillis declared firmly.

"Me neither," Yates added.

Everyone but Stan Auerbach. Dave

shifted his gaze to the rancher, bobbed his head. "I'll have my crew cut out your stock in the morning, and drive them into that sink west of the corrals. You can head them back onto your range anytime you like."

Auerbach, face taut, said: "Don't go to no trouble. I'll send my boys over first thing, get them out of your way."

"Suit yourself . . . One thing more, I'd like to keep this all quiet. Expect Farman's got riders watching all of us and keeping an eye on the Flat, too. As soon not tip him off to what we're doing until the last minute."

"Not much of a chance hiding it from him," Wheeler said. "Minute you head out across the Flat, he'll know."

"Won't be doing it exactly that way right off. Aim to trail the herd south along the edge until dark. Hadn't exactly planned it that way but, turning out like it has, I figure it'll be smart."

Drury grinned. "See what you mean. You're giving him the idea that you're going around the Flat, like he told us."

Bradford said, "What I hope. It'll cost me ten miles but it'll be worth it if I can throw them off. Could be when I swing east the next morning there won't be anybody watching."

"And maybe you'll get clear across be-fore Farman gets wise to it," Gillis said. "Trick could work."

"Like to think it will." Bradford reached into his pocket, produced the leather fold in which he had placed the necessary bills of sale the ranchers had given him when they had driven in their cattle earlier that week. Thumbing though them, he singled out Auerbach's and handed it to him.

The rancher folded it across, tucked it into a pocket and stared hard at Dave. "No hard feelings?"

"No. Man has to do what he thinks is best. Maybe I don't agree with you but I respect your right to make your own decisions."

Bradford turned away to the other men now moving off into the dusk for their waiting horses.

"Like to say it again — any of you want to change your mind after you've slept on it, I'll understand . . . Just let me know in the morning so's I can cut out your stock."

"Be no change far as I'm concerned," Nate Wheeler said. "Good luck."

The others echoed Nate's sentiments and continued on, their voices low in the afternoon quiet. Auerbach, not moving, studied Dave quietly.

"Reckon you know this could cost you

more than the herd you'll be driving," he said. "Farman don't keep hothands like Casey and Macklin on the payroll because he likes them."

Bradford shrugged. "Not something I don't already know, Stan."

"And if it comes to a showdown you know goddam well there'll be none of them coming to stand by you — not even Wheeler."

"I see it different. Maybe some of them will back off but not all. They're admitting to themselves that their future is at stake in this."

"What future? Even if you make it across Texas Flat and sell the herd in Wichita, and come back with all the money — Farman's not going to let it drop! He'll hit you and every rancher in the Cebolla Basin — and hit hard."

Bradford glanced again to the sun, now slipping behind the hills to the west. "Chances are you're right, but it's a hill I'll climb when I come to it. Important thing to me — to all of us taking a hand — is making that drive across the Flat and letting Farman know that he couldn't scare us off, keep us from doing it . . . What comes afterwards is another verse . . . Good night."

Abruptly Dave Bradford wheeled, started for the house. Auerbach remained where he stood for a long breath, and then sighing, murmured, "Good night — and luck," and walked on to his horse.

4

He could be leading the ranchers of the Basin into a hell of a lot of trouble, Bradford thought later that evening as he sat alone on the bench he'd built under one of the cottonwoods in his yard. He went there often when he had problems and wanted to think.

The night was still and warm and the smell of summer was in the air relieving, finally, the subtle chill that winter, reluctant as always to surrender, had laid upon the spring months.

The owl that nested in the barn rushed by on softly swishing wings and back on the slopes of the Shadow Mountains, coyotes barked into the starlight. Two small eyes, like live coals, glowed at him from the side of the house where a lamp laid a yellow rectangle through a window into the yard . . . *Skunk,* he thought, and then moments later watched the white-striped little animal hurriedly off into nearby brush.

He stirred restlessly, reached for his

makings and began to roll a cigarette. He was wishing now that Wheeler and the other ranchers had followed Auerbach's example and withdrawn their cattle leaving him with only his own stock to worry about on the drive.

None of them could afford to lose their steers, the small ranchers particularly. Wheeler could probably survive, as would he, but the rest . . . He groaned, swore quietly. He'd gotten so wrapped up in the principle of the thing that he guessed he'd overlooked being practical, leastwise where they were concerned.

Maybe by morning some of them would have had second thoughts about it and decide to stay clear of the conflict building up between him and JJ Farman. He'd made the suggestion, given them that option, and they'd refused. But if they would all show up, declare they felt it best not to become involved, he'd actually like it better. For himself, he'd not turn back, not if —

His thoughts came to a stop as the measured beat of a loping horse reached him. The rider was coming up from the south, following the road that ran the Basin from top to bottom and led to the settlement of King's Crossing which lay at its lower end.

Dave listened thoughtfully, wondering who would be riding north at that hour of the night, and then as the thudding drew nearer, slowed, a smile split his long lips. He got to his feet. It was Sirral Drury.

He stepped away from the bench, showed himself, and she veered the pony toward him. He caught the animal's head-stall, halted it, and then moved to the girl's side and helped her dismount. Together they returned to the bench.

"Was hoping to see you," he said as they sat down.

She smiled up at him. "I intended to wait until morning but changed my mind."

"Glad you did . . . Feel like talking?"

Sirral's face was a pale oval in the sil-vered night, and around it her honey-colored hair was like a halo. "Is there trouble already?"

"No — no trouble. Just thinking a bit about the others I've maybe dragged into this. Your pa — Wheeler, all the rest. Sorry now I talked them into it."

"I don't think you did," the girl replied with a shake of her head. "I know you didn't Pa. You just made him see what backing down to Farman would mean. It was his own choice whether to knuckle under or not."

"But if I hadn't made that stand against Farman none of us would be faced with —"

"Could you have done anything else?" she broke in quietly.

Bradford gave that a long minute of thought. "No, reckon not," he said finally. "Just can't swallow that kind of a deal. Seen too many of the Farman kind and I know what they can do to a country."

"Then you've no reason to be sorry, Dave. You only did what you knew was right and had to do."

He shifted restlessly. "Expect that's what's eating at me — doing what I felt I had to do. I'm risking my neck and my ranch and there's a damned good chance I could lose both — which is all right for me. But something keeps telling me I was wrong to suck others in on it."

"Why not? It's their Basin, too, same as it's their future . . . And you didn't suck them in. Pa said Stan Auerbach wouldn't side in with you. The others had the same chance — and didn't take it."

"Maybe because they were afraid of what the rest would think."

"That didn't stop Stan —"

"Well, Auerbach's — Auerbach. Everybody sort of expects him to be that way." Dave paused, came half around, and taking

Sirral's shoulders in his broad hands, looked closely at her.

"If this turns out wrong and I end up with nothing, it'll mean our plans will be gone, too . . . You know that, don't you?"

She leaned forward, pecked him with a light kiss. "No matter how it turns out, nothing will change between us . . . You're the one who's wanted to wait, hold off until you got everything all fixed up just right."

"I only wanted you to have the best —"

"I know that, but it isn't necessary, Dave. I don't have to have all those fine things."

"I figure you do. I won't have you grubbing your life away like some of the women I see around here."

"They live though it, and so could I . . . But it won't come to that. I'm not afraid of you failing — and when you come back the whole Basin will owe you a debt of gratitude . . . But even if you do lose your herd we'll have enough left to get by — start over again. We can go somewhere else if it has to be that way."

"Could be how it'll work out if things go completely wrong. But I'm not planning on that happening, not while I can still use a gun."

Sirral lowered her head. "That's what

worries me, Dave — that part of it. I know you can take care of yourself, that you're better than most if it comes down to shooting. Pa has told us about Abilene and Dodge City and all those other places where you were a lawman or a guard or had some kind of a job where you had to depend on your gun.

"But Farman has a dozen killers he can send against you and try to stop you with. With so many — how —"

"Learned a long time ago never to bite off more than I can chew. And I won't be alone. I'll have five good men with me . . . Anyway, don't fret over that. I like living and since I came here, met you, I've got too much to lose."

She was silent for a time, and then, lips tight, she shook her head. "I'll not worry about it. I know you can take care of yourself and that you'll come back to me . . . I feel it . . . How long will you be gone?"

"Little over a month, I expect. It's a long drive but I don't reckon it'll be as tough as some I've made."

"That means it will be June when you get back," she murmured, and then turned to him impulsively. "When you do let's go ahead — get married, Dave. Let's not wait any longer."

He frowned. "No matter how things have panned out?"

"I've already said that it didn't matter . . . It wouldn't be too hard. You could start over with the ranch again and I'd keep on teaching. The families pay me a dollar a month for each child and I have sixteen in my class now. Besides, I've a little money saved —"

"Your money — not ours," he said gruffly. "You are to use it on yourself."

"It could be for us," she corrected, "but I don't think we'll need it. Everything will turn out all right."

"Sure," he said. "It's got to."

She rose to her feet, still holding to his hand. He followed, and together they walked slowly toward her pony.

"I won't see you again until you're back," she murmured.

"Reckon not. Aim to pull out right after noon and there's quite a bit to be done in the morning first. Glad you came by this evening. I'd planned to ride over to your place first chance I got."

"It's easier to talk here," she replied, halting. Abruptly she turned, threw her arms about him. He held her close for a time and then picking her up easily, placed her on the mare's saddle.

"Best you go," he said.

She took up the reins, smiled. Leaning over, she kissed him squarely, murmured, "Good-bye," and swung the pony away.

Bradford echoed her words, and moving deeper into the yard, watched until he could see her and the white pony no longer, and then turned toward the house . . . He could afford to lose everything but Sirral Drury.

5

Two of Auerbach's hired hands were already on the job that next morning when Dave reached the swale where the gather had been bedded down. Assigning Sam Zulinski and Claude Jackson to assist them in cutting out the steers bearing Auerbach's Circle A brand, he set about checking the preparations made for the long trek to Wichita, and wondering, hopefully if there would be others in the Basin who had undergone a change of mind and would be coming for their stock.

His own thinking on the matter had, if anything, become more resolute. The conversation with Sirral Drury had somehow served to crystallize his determination to an even greater extent, and the venture had assumed an aspect of make-or-break as far as he was concerned.

But the others in Cebolla Basin — he shook his head irritably as he rode slowly around the mixed herd; he could weather loss and defeat if such developed, the rest of the ranchers and homesteaders, with the possible exception of Nate Wheeler, could not and he knew he would never rid himself of a feeling of guilt should he fail them.

Late in the morning he saw Milt Fresno on the seat of the chuck wagon moving down the slope from the ranch. At once he rode back to the house for a few final words with one of the punchers who was remaining behind after which he made his inquiry as to whether any of the other ranchers had been by.

Claussen, a balding oldster with a tobacco-stained, stringy mustache, brushed at the sweat on his beet-red face, shook his head. "Nope, nary a one. Who was you expecting?"

"All of them, I hoped."

Claussen gave him a puzzled look. "That mean you wanted them all to back out — like Auerbach?"

Dave nodded. "I'd feel better if I was risking just my own beef."

The old rider hawked, spat into the dust. "See what you're meaning, but I reckon they figure they've got as much to gain as you."

Bradford grinned. Claussen had stated the proposition from the positive side

45

rather than the negative, and it made him feel better. Reaching down, he shook the man's hand and wheeled away.

"Have a care," the oldster called after him.

Bradford bobbed his head and pointed for the swale. A distance off to his right he could see Auerbach's men driving the Circle A herd toward the southwest. One thing definite could be said about Stan; he'd never lose out because of a gamble — he was one who always played it safe.

Dave gave that thought. Perhaps that was the way a man ought to be — careful, cautious to the point of not taking any risks. He shrugged, reckoned it might be all right for some but he couldn't live that way. A man had to take a chance now and then if he expected to ever reach the top.

The crew had the herd in a tight cluster when Dave again rode into the hollow. Fresno, his wagon drawn up under a sycamore on the west side, had broken out sandwiches he had prepared for the noon lunch and had coffee on the fire. The four riders who would be making the drive were hunched in the shade under the tree, munching their bread and meat while sipping black liquid from tin cups.

Jackson rose to meet him as he swung down. "Can move out anytime you say."

Bradford accepted a sandwich and cup from Milt Fresno. "Soon as we eat."

Jackson nodded, helped himself to a refill from the simmering pot. "Way I understand you, we head south 'til we come to Coyote Creek, and bed 'em down there for the night."

"What I've got in mind . . . I figure we ought to reach there by dark."

"Just about. Then, come morning, you aim to cut east across Texas Flat?"

"That's it," Bradford said.

Claude Jackson, a tall, cotton-haired man in his late thirties who served as Spur's foreman, studied the liquid in his cup in silence.

Dave eyed him narrowly. "You think I'm wrong?"

Jackson's shoulders twitched. "Wrong or not, it's you calling the turn."

Dave finished his sandwich, washed it down with a final swallow of coffee. Moving to the opposite side of the fire, he faced the rest of the crew.

"Any of you worrying about crossing the Flat?"

Zulinski wagged his head. "Not me . . . All in the day's work."

Dave shifted his eyes to Ruskin and Miller. "You?"

Both men shrugged. Ruskin said, "If there's trouble, there's trouble. I don't aim to get overhet worrying about it."

"I'm hoping to avoid it. Pretty sure Farman's got us watched so, if we move south, steering wide of the Flat today it could throw him off, get him to thinking we're taking the trail through the brakes. That should cause him to pull off his spies."

"Sure a good chance of it," Ruskin said. "How long'll it take us to cross Texas Flat?"

"Four days, a bit more maybe. Once we reach the Satanta River — about three days — we ought to be in the clear." Bradford's attention went to Jackson, quiet through the exchange. "Not forcing any man to make the drive. Thought I made that plain at the start. Any of you wants to pull out, now's the time to do it."

Spur's foreman stirred, feeling the eyes of the crew as well as those of Bradford upon him. "Not aiming to pull out, just want to be sure of what I'm up against. There extra cartridges to be had?"

"Plenty. In the wagon," Dave replied.

"Good enough," Jackson said. Tossing his empty cup to Fresno, he glanced about.

"All right, shake your shanks. Them steers ain't going to start by themselves."

A half hour later the herd was underway, Jackson riding point, Zulinski, Ruskin and Earl Miller drifting back and forth from swing to drag while Bradford, acting in the capacity of an outrider, roamed the country ahead keeping out of the dust churned up by the cattle in order to keep watch for any suspicious riders who might be in the area.

Milt Fresno, the string of spare horses trailing along behind his wagon, had swung to the east side of the herd, also avoiding the rolling clouds of powdery dust. It was likely such position actually put him on Texas Flat but Bradford dismissed the fact; as long as the cattle were seen pointing south, JJ Farman would take no offense.

The herd traveled well. They had grazed, watered, and rested for a full day and a half before the drive began and were in a mood to trail if a bit erratic in the doing. But shortly after the start an old brindle steer, wearing Calvin Yates's C-Bar-Y brand, horned his way to the fore and took over leadership. From that point on there was no breaking rank and straying, the rest of the herd seemingly content to follow the brindle unquestioningly.

They reached Coyote Creek well before sundown. Jackson and his crew, showing the results of their long experience in such matters, herded the cattle into a convenient hollow along which the small stream cut a narrow path and quickly had them settled for the night.

By the time they had finished their chore Fresno had a meal of fried meat and potatoes sided by Dutch oven biscuits, honey and coffee ready, and all turned to for supper. Later, with a man posted to each of the four sides of the swale where he could catch his forty winks while still more or less on night watch, Dave Bradford mounted and rode a short distance out onto Texas Flat.

It was an endless silver-tinted carpet stretching as far as the eye could see to the east under a three-quarter moon and a vast spray of stars. He could see no red eye of a campfire anywhere on the limitless expanse and that gave him a feeling of relief. It could only mean that none of Farman's riders were maintaining surveillance.

He had seen no riders during the long afternoon but such was no assurance they were not about. He was certain in his mind that Farman had kept the herd under observation; therefore the absence of a night camp would indicate that his men had pulled out, satisfied that he was not cutting across the plains of Texas Flat, and would so report to the rancher.

That was good. It was as he had hoped . . . But tomorrow was another day — a day in which they actually would be on the Flat. He could only hope that riders from the J-Bar-J would not drop back for a second look. If so, trouble would begin early.

6

The soft black velvet of the sky became overcast during the night as heavy clouds rolled in from the south. Beyond the Shadow Mountains lightning occasionally slashed a jagged path through the curtain and thunder rumbled threateningly.

But no rain developed and shortly before the sun appeared behind a dull gray shield in the east, Bradford and his riders had the herd up and moving. A shower would be welcome. It would break the heat that had lain across the Cebolla Basin for several weeks, and it would hold down the thirst of the cattle — due to wait until the Satanta was reached before they could water again.

The morning wore on, however, with no more than a quick splatter of drops that ended quickly and by noon broad patches of blue had begun to appear overhead.

As before Dave rode well in front of the herd, keeping sharp watch on the long plains, particularly those to the north

"Expect they did figure the way the boss was hoping — that we was heading for the brakes. Now, if they'll just keep on thinking that —"

Dave, on the farther side of the vehicle swapping tack from the buckskin he'd ridden that day onto a tall sorrel, paused at the chore.

"Good chance they will. Don't think Farman runs any cattle this far south of his place on the Flat. Running into any of his riders now will be pure accident."

"Unless somebody spots the dust," Jackson said.

"Ain't been much of that," Ruskin commented. "And the grass is pretty thick and the ground ain't loose even if it is dry."

"Rain'll help, if it'll only come."

"It won't," Fresno said flatly. "Them ain't wet clouds we're seeing, just the promising kind."

Bradford, inclined to believe the old cook's estimation of possibilities, resumed his labors of making ready the sorrel. A hard rain would be a lucky break, not only keep down the light cloud of dust that hovered over the moving cattle but would keep them in a good frame of mind as well.

Of course, one of the wild, electrical storms that occasionally struck that part of the country — they could do without. While the herd was small — five hundred and sixty-five head to be exact — the crew and he would have little trouble in keeping a stampede running in the right direction, but he did not relish the thought of losses that would occur, or the weight the frightened animals would run off.

He'd like to think of reaching Wichita with the herd intact, something that would border on the edge of a miracle, but it would be a fine thing, nevertheless, and something sure to make a successful crossing of Texas Flat even more of a victory.

The steers, tired after the first full day of trailing, rested quietly throughout the night. Getting them underway the next morning proved to be a trifle more difficult than previously, but once Jackson had the old brindle out where he could be seen, and moving, the rest fell into line.

The day, a mixture of hot sun, scudding, dry clouds and choking dust, proved to be little different from the first. Dave ranged farther north in his outrider duties, pointing at one time for a low run of bubble-like hills from which he would be afforded a good view of the country surrounding them.

He spent a long hour on the crest of the

highest, examining the Flat in all directions — and saw nothing other than a few jackrabbits and a solitary coyote skulking about in the chamisa. Evidently Farman was satisfied they had pushed the herd on to the south and were taking the cattle through the brakes, otherwise they would have encountered J-Bar-J riders before that hour.

Repeating such to his crew that night when they had finished bedding down the cattle and gathered for supper, brought a noticeable relief to all. Even Claude Jackson, definitely on the alert from the morning they had turned east onto the Flat, appeared to relax.

"Reckon it's going to work out," he said, wrapping his hands around a cup of coffee. "Was we to have trouble sure seems it would've come before now."

Dave nodded but he was making no concession. He'd not feel the danger was over until they had reached the far side of Texas Flat, still two full days or more away — assuming all continued to go well and there were no unexpected delays.

"Best we don't let down just the same," he said. "Looks good, I'll admit but we won't be out of the woods until we're all the way across and heading onto the Wichita Trail."

"You figure we ought to keep posting night guards like we've been doing?" Miller asked. "This here sleeping with one eye open's about to catch up with me."

Bradford nodded. "Something we'd best plan on doing all the way to the railhead . . . Can maybe cut it down to taking turns, however, once we're on the Trail."

"Then you ain't so sure after all that we're in the clear?" Jackson said, frowning.

"Won't be certain until those steers are in the pens at Wichita and I'm on my way to the bank with a buyer's draft — that's how I feel about it."

Milt Fresno laughed. "And that's when I'm going to buy myself a quart of redeye and swaller it down without taking ary a breath!" he said. "How about you, Sam Zu?"

"Amen," the puncher replied feelingly.

Bradford glanced at his men curiously. They had felt the pressure of the drive far more than they had let on, he realized. All had made him feel that it would be little more than any ordinary day's work, that they were unworried to any extent over the possibility of exchanging bullets with Farman's hired hands. Only Claude Jackson had been unable to entirely conceal his inner doubts.

Dave felt a warmness flow through him for these men who were riding at his side. When it was all over he'd figure out some way to show his appreciation.

"Expect we'll be reaching that river to-morrow late," Zulinski said, rising and moving to the wagon for his blanket. "Sure would be nice to spend a day laying over, doing nothing — not that I'm asking. Just saying it would be mighty nice."

Dave only smiled, knowing what the puncher meant. But it was out of the question. Perhaps, when they reached the Wichita Trail they could hold up for a day at some settlement. Then men would all be ready for a night off and it wouldn't hurt to rest the cattle.

The next day was much like the second, only with an utterly cloudless sky from which the sun bore down intensely. By noon the herd had become sullen and hard to handle and Bradford breathed a prayer of thanks for the Satanta River which now was only a few hours distant. Once there the steers would quiet down.

They caught sight of the Satanta, a fairly good stream cutting its way through the low hills, about midafternoon, and not long after that a shifting breeze carried the smell of it to the herd. The cattle reacted at once, slowing their pace while they tested the air with dust filmed nostrils, and then abruptly breaking into a run.

Bradford, riding across the front of the surging mass, waved off Miller. "Let 'em run! They'll stop when they hit the river . . . Tell Sam Zu!"

He saw the rider wheel away, race to relay the order to Zulinski not far beyond him, and then dropped back to the opposite side of the herd in search of Jackson and Earl Ruskin.

He made the crossover well ahead of the steers, loping easily but not plunging on blindly as they would be if stampeding, and broke through the wall of dust on that side.

He saw first Claude Jackson's riderless horse and pulled up short. An instant later he had a glimpse of a dozen or so riders sweeping through the short hills now behind the herd. They were spreading out to form a half circle, their guns crackling hollowly above the thudding of the running steers . . . He had not fooled Farman after all.

7

Anger lifted within Dave Bradford, settled into a deadly sort of calmness. Drawing his pistol, he dug spurs into the sorrel, sent the big gelding rushing toward Farman's riders. Gunshots were a steady sound faintly audible above the thunder of the herd.

Abruptly Earl Ruskin broke out of the dust. His hat was gone. A dark stain had spread over his left side and his arm hung limply from the shoulder. He was guiding his horse with his knees, using his right hand to fire at the oncoming riders.

Bradford yelled at the man to pull off, to get clear of the fighting, and opened up with his own weapon. Ruskin turned a sweat- and dust-smeared face to him, grinned tautly, and rode on, ignoring the order.

Two of the raiders curved off from the main party, swerved in to meet Dave. Crouched low on the saddle, Bradford steadied his weapon on his left forearm, pressed off a shot. Then man to his right jolted, straightened and immediately swung away, head bobbling loosely.

His partner cut back to the opposite directly hurriedly, roweling his horse savagely. Dave threw a shot at him, missed, cursed when the hammer of his .45 came down on an empty cartridge.

He hauled in on the leathers, slowed the sorrel to a walk as he thumbed fresh shells from his belt, rodded the empties from the pistol's cylinder. The herd had quickened its pace, spurred by the racket of the guns, he realized.

They should be nearing the Satanta, but now a doubt as to whether they would stop or not was entering Dave's mind. Badly frightened, there was a good possibility they would keep running . . . But the river could also prove to be a death trap; if the steers in the lead did halt, those following, unaware of the fact, would plow into them and wholesale slaughter would result.

A bullet whipped at Bradford's sleeve. Another struck the saddle with a dull thump. He jammed the last shell into its chamber, snapped the loading gate shut and spurred ahead.

Dust was now a thick, choking curtain that enclosed him. He could see none of the raiders, knew the location of the running cattle only from the sound of their pounding hoofs. The gunshots had not lessened, and cutting the sorrel hard left, he pointed into the direction in which the shooting appeared to be the heaviest.

The odds were bad — worse even now than at the start. Claude Jackson had evidently been shot from the saddle. Ruskin was wounded, perhaps by that moment, was dead. He had no idea of what had taken place on the opposite flank of the herd where he had last seen Zulinski and Miller — and Milt Fresno . . . They could all be out of it by now, too.

Grim, he urged the gelding to a hard gallop, sliced diagonally through the dense folds of choking tan for the far side of the herd. A rider loomed up before him — a man wearing a sweat-stained white hat, and with a bandanna drawn tight over the lower half of his face to mask off the dust.

The raider's eyes flared at the sudden confrontation. His gun came up, blossomed smoke in the same fragment of time that Bradford triggered his bullet. The man flinched, clawed at his shoulder and spun off into the yellow haze, gone before Dave could get off a second shot.

Bradford broke into the open in the next

moment. Off to the west a steady racket of shooting drew his instant attention. Glancing that way he saw Fresno and the chuck wagon, closely pursued by three riders, racing across the flat.

The old cook had braced himself in the seat, legs spread, booted feet jammed against the dashboard. The reins of the madly running team were wrapped about the whipstock while Fresno, shotgun in his hands, blasted away at the men. His weapon was ineffectual at the range separating him from the raiders who were hanging back, coolly awaiting their chance.

Anger again rocked Dave Bradford. The sight of the three killers relentlessly closing in on the near helpless old man, trapped between them, unable to protect himself to any extent, sent him surging forward on the sorrel, gun firing steadily, curses streaming from his lips.

The raiders paid no heed. The clanking and banging of the wagon as it bounced and lurched over the ground, the thudding of their own horses' hoofs, plus the sporadic booming of the shotgun drowned the sound of Dave's approach.

He saw nothing of Sam Zulinski or Miller — nor of Earl Ruskin either who most certainly was now off his saddle either dead or badly wounded. The pall of dust surrounding the herd, now seemingly slowing, shut off view of all except the fleeing chuck wagon and the men pursuing it.

Suddenly the wagon veered, began to sway and skid from side to side. Fresno dropped the shotgun, caught at the seat handles to save himself from being pitched to the ground. A shout went up from the rider immediately behind the vehicle, and leaning forward, he emptied his pistol at the sloughing wagon.

At that instant he saw Bradford. His head came up, eyes widened as he looked into Dave's leveled weapon. Sawing at the bit, he cut his horse hard left, paused as Bradford's bullet slammed into him. He raised an arm, as if to protest, knocked his hat off, and then tumbled to the ground.

Without a second look, Dave veered to overtake the man farther on. His glance came about just as the wagon upended, and with furiously spinning wheels, came down upon its canvas top. One of the horses had taken a bullet, gone down, tripping up his teammate and catapulting the vehicle.

Bradford yelled, eyes searching anxiously for Milt Fresno. He saw the slight figure of

the old cook crumpled into a dusty heap just beyond the dead horse, and spurred toward it, firing as he went. The raider to his left wheeled, finally aware of his presence. Dave snapped a hasty shot at him, missed.

Cursing, he cut the sorrel away sharply, triggered another bullet. The raider on the far side of the wrecked chuck wagon was now curving in, weapon aimed, dark features intent. Bradford pressed off a shot at him — the last in his pistol. The rider flinched, but came on.

Jaw set, Dave roweled the sorrel deep, sent him straight on toward the man while he pushed cartridges from their loops in a hurried effort to reload. He got two shells into the cylinder, frowned as he saw other riders racing in from the side, all firing at him. Beyond the puffs of smoke he saw the blurred but recognizable faces of two he knew — Casey and Guy Macklin.

Anger and hatred flamed through him He brought up his weapon, fired hurriedly In that next instant a tremendous force smashed into the side of his head. He ha a fleeting glimpse of riders swarming about him, and then all was in blackness

8

Dave Bradford fought his way back slowly to consciousness. He was only vaguely aware that it was cool and the land around him lay in silence, bathed in the pale glow of moonlight.

He remained motionless for several long minutes, eyes staring up into the silver speckled sky while he struggled to remember, to collect his scattered senses. A groan slipped from his lips as it all came rushing into his mind.

They had been raided by Farman's hired hands. Kurt Casey and Guy Macklin had been with them, were undoubtedly the leaders. The herd, running for the river, had stampeded when the shooting began. Both Jackson and Ruskin had been shot . . . And Milt Fresno . . . Dave stirred as the recollection of what had been taking place when a bullet had felled him . . . Three of the riders had been after the old cook. The chuck wagon had overturned in

its wild flight across the Flat. He had tried to help — had been too late. And then he had gone down.

Abruptly he sat up. The quick movement sent a spasm of pain stabbing through his head which in turn summoned a wave of nausea. Face tipped down, he hung motionless until the sickness passed and then slowly looked up.

It was night. He must have lain where he fell for hours. Brushing at his face dazedly, he picked up his pistol half-hidden under one leg, holstered it and drew himself upright. Pain again slugged him. He paused, on his feet but swaying unsteadily.

He raised his hand, probed the numbed side of his head. A crust covered it and there appeared to be a broad patch of swelling. He withdrew his fingers hastily at the tenderness, recalling as he did that it had been a bullet from Casey's gun that had downed him. Fortunately he had only been grazed and knocked cold. He guessed he should consider himself lucky to be alive.

The unsteadiness in his legs persisted as he traveled his gaze around. He could see a dark mass a few yards below him, assumed it to be the wrecked chuck wagon. One horse stood silhouetted nearby. Other than that he was alone in a vast, quiet world.

Gathering his strength he made his way to the vehicle, becoming aware as he drew nearer of the smell of charred wood, cloth and the stench of scorched flesh and hair. Halting, he stared at the blackened mound. Embers still glowed among the ruin. Evidently the raiders had set fire to the wagon after it had capsized. It had burned almost completely, only the metal parts yet remaining. The odor came from the dead horse that had been partly trapped beneath it.

Fresno . . .

Impulsively he lurched toward the figure lying a few paces to one side and crouched beside it. The old man was dead — one bullet hole in his back, another in his left side.

A hard, throbbing anger flowing through him, overriding the steady pain in his head, Dave Bradford brought himself upright again and stared out over the land. There had been no need to kill Fresno. He was only doing a job, the same as Jackson and the others. Driving them off would have been sufficient but Casey and Macklin had exacted more than the necessary price.

Price . . . He had paid one hell of a price himself in his attempt to buck JJ Farman

. . . Five men — the entire herd of cattle — all the horses — everything gone. He had failed completely.

Slowly he came back around, gaze again on Milt Fresno as a coldness claimed him. Farman's men had made one mistake; they had thought him dead, too. Only he wasn't. Far from it — and as long as he lived he'd not have another moment's peace until he had squared up with Macklin and Casey and Farman, and all the others involved. He could do nothing about returning to life the men who had been shot down but he could do plenty in making those responsible pay for what they had done.

The herd was a different matter. He must do what he could to recover it — somehow. It would be a hell of a big job — one man against many, and if successful, he would be faced with a continuation of the drive to a point still weeks in the distance, alone. He shook his head considering the task. Impossible — but he'd try nevertheless. He'd manage it somehow. Perhaps he could get help somewhere.

His hand dropped to the pistol at his hip. He drew the weapon, reloaded it absently, eyes still on the dusty lump of cloth that was Milt Fresno. The herd had probably halted at the river and was there yet. Casey and those who had not been hurt in the raid would be close by, gloating over their success. Likely they planned to drive the stock onto Farman range, rebrand them with a J-Bar-J iron, and add them to the rancher's already large herd.

Or they could be keeping them for themselves, a bonus from Farman, figuring to continue the drive to Wichita, sell out to the first buyer who wasn't too particular about legal ownership and split the proceeds.

No matter which, they'd have him to reckon with before they did anything. Meanwhile, he had other matters to attend to — that of seeing to the burial of Fresno and the other members of the crew if he could locate their bodies. Casey and his followers would still be there when morning came.

The unsteadiness almost gone, Bradford crossed to the remains of the wagon. Several items had been thrown clear when it overturned and if he was lucky, he would find the spade that was always carried. He came upon the old cook's canteen first and halting, picked it up. It was half full. Unscrewing the cap, he soaked his bandanna, bathed his face and removed the crust of blood stiffening the skin around the wound Casey's grazing bullet had left.

The cleansing made him feel better, and hanging the container over his shoulder, he resumed the search. The spade was not among the articles that had been spilled from the wagon. IIc found it sometime later in the blackened remains; the handle had been burned away.

Kicking the pointed scoop clear, he permitted it to cool and then picking it up he returned to where Fresno lay. Holding the spade head in both hands, he gouged and scraped out a trench from the firm soil alongside the man, and when it was deep enough, placed him in it.

He had no blanket with which to cover the body, simply replaced the dirt, forming a mound. Then, taking a partly destroyed spoke from one of the wheels, he thrust it into the head of the grave as a marker. Sometime later, perhaps, he would return and do a better job of it for Milt. At the moment such precautions against the buzzards and coyotes would have to suffice.

Keeping the spade head, he walked to where the surviving team horse stood trapped in his trailing harness. The animal, frightened by the overturning wagon and subsequent fire, had broken his trace and run, only to have the dangling leather straps become entangled in a clump of juniper.

It was a break for him, Dave realized, for otherwise he would have been left on foot. The sorrel he had been riding had evidently continued on with the herd and the fleeing remuda as horses often do when confused.

Taking his knife, Dave cut through the harness remnants, leaving only the bridle and a short length of reins. It had been years since he'd done any amount of riding without a saddle, but he had no choice now, and heaving himself onto the broad back of the still skittish black, he brought him around and crossed to where he figured he should find the bodies of Ruskin and Claude Jackson.

He came upon Jackson almost at once, accorded him the same simple rites as he had visited on Milt Fresno. It required another two hours to locate Ruskin, however; the puncher had pulled himself up under a clump of rabbit brush where he had evidently made a last ditch stand.

The hard digging with the scoop set Bradford's head to throbbing sickeningly, and when Ruskin was finally underground, he sat back to rest and allow the pain to subside. As he waited the hard, fierce determination to bring Casey and Macklin and Farman to account again possessed him. It was now a personal matter. The need to drive a herd across Texas Flat and disprove JJ Farman's invincibility was of secondary importance in his mind; making them pay for the murders of his crew came first.

His breathing normal again, the pain in his head at low pulse, Bradford got wearily to his feet and climbed back onto the gelding. He should get on with the grisly chore of burying the others; he needed to reach the Satanta before daylight. It came to him then as he settled onto the black, that he had come across none of the raiders during his search. Several had been hit by his bullets, he knew — one of which he was positive had been killed.

The only answer was that the outlaws had taken their dead and wounded with them, not wishing to leave any of their number behind for fear of linking JJ Farman with the raid.

Raking the horse with his spurs, he headed back to the blackened spot that marked the position of the destroyed wagon and turned east, beginning his search for Sam Zulinski and Rufe Miller from that point. He had last seen them in that general direction.

Three hours later he drew to a halt and slid to the ground to ease the aching muscles of his legs and back. He had found no sign of the two men although he had whipped back and forth over a broad expanse of the plain in a careful inspection. The bodies simply weren't there.

It could only mean one of two things; either the pair had fled before the raiders when they saw the hopelessness of the situation or Casey and the others had taken them prisoner. Dave shook his head as he considered the latter.

Such wasn't likely. Farman's men would want no one left alive to bear witness, thus a prisoner would be most undesirable. It had to be that the two punchers had ridden on to escape the death they saw befalling their partners. He guessed he shouldn't blame them — but if they could have all gotten together and made a stand, the situation might have ended differently.

It was too late to think of that. He was the sole survivor to what amounted to a massacre — evidently — and it was up to him to go ahead with plans to do something about it.

Head throbbing, weariness lying upon

his shoulders in a solid, heavy mass, he turned his gaze to the direction of the river. There was no hint of daylight yet in the velvet sky beyond the eastern hills, but first light could not be long away. He should be moving in close, gaining a position where he could watch Casey and his men — and the herd — and figure out what he could do.

Roweling the black once more, he sent the horse forward at a fast pace, keeping well below the path the stampeding herd had taken. It would not due to blunder straight into the men and the cattle; best to approach the river at a safe distance from them, then work his way upstream to where he could observe.

He reached the shallow canyon through which the stream flowed an hour later and rode down into the quietly running water. The black was thirsty after the long day and wild night, and lowered his head at once, began to suck in great gulps of water. Dave dismounted, again bathed his face and head to refresh himself, and then emptying Milt Fresno's canteen filled it with the cool water.

He turned then, and leading the gelding along the spongy bank, struck upstream, ears alert for sounds of the cattle. He continued on for a full hour, while a growing worry mounted within him. When daylight finally broke across the land, he knew for certain that which had been a suspicion was a fact; the herd was not along the river.

9

Puzzled, Dave Bradford dropped from his horse and stared upstream, following the slightly twisting course of the water with his eyes until a sharp bend finally closed it off to view.

He turned, looked to the opposite direction, frowned. He had not bothered to look for tracks earlier, believing there was no need; he had been positive he would find the cattle and the men who had stolen them along the river. He swung his attention to the moist banks of the stream, near level with the flat in this particular area. There were no hoofprints. Dave shrugged impatiently. It made no sense.

Climbing onto the gelding, he wheeled about and retraced his path along the river, eyes on the ground. A time later he drew up. The soil was marked by a welter of tracks. Dismounting he made a fairly close examination; here was where the cattle had entered the water after their flight across the flat.

It was apparent they had not remained there for long. There were few droppings, although it was likely much of it could have been washed away. Still, it was reasonable to expect more sign.

But that was a problem of small consequence: What had happened to the herd? Five hundred and sixty-five steers just couldn't vanish from the face of the earth!

Wondering, Bradford doubled back onto the flat. The ground was firm, covered by a tough, wiry grass that showed little trace of the herd's passage. Here and there he noted a deep gouge where a sharp hoof had cut into the sod, an occasional trampled bush, but on the whole there was not too much visible proof of the path the rushing cattle had followed.

Regardless, the moist, sloping edge of the stream revealed where the herd had entered the water; accordingly, it was only reasonable to believe that the place where the steers had been driven from it would also be apparent.

Mounting, Bradford rode south for a full mile, found nothing. Reversing himself, he went upriver, eyes now probing the shore line carefully. He reached the point where he had first halted, again stopped . . . It simply didn't add up; he had not found a place where the herd had left the stream.

Irritated with himself, and more puzzled now than earlier, he pulled away from the Satanta and rode the black to the crest of a low hill a quarter mile back on the flat. That Casey and his outlaw friends had moved the cattle off the river was evident — but where? And what had they done with them?

On the top of the rise he turned his glance to the north — into the direction in which the J-Bar-J lay. A grunt of satisfaction slipped from his tight lips. Several miles in the distance a dark mass filling a swale indicated the location of a herd.

Riding off the hill at once, he loped the black to a point where he could dismount and work in close. Leaving the gelding tied to a cedar, he followed out a narrow draw and approached the herd from its lower side, and halted.

Two riders squatted near their horses on the opposite slope of the shallow basin. Keeping the steers between himself and the pair, Dave hunched low and hurried to where he was within only strides of the grazing herd.

He pulled up short, disappointment and frustration running though him. These weren't his steers. On the hip of each one visible to him was the bold J-Bar-J brand of the Farman spread. It was simply another of the rancher's numerous herds.

He swore quietly, turned, made his way back to his horse. The mystery was now more baffling than ever — but he knew there was a logical explanation, knew also that he must find it.

Going onto the black, he sat for a time staring out toward Texas Flat. Maybe he was going at it all wrong; maybe he should return to the Cebolla Basin, recruit the aid of the other ranchers and make a thorough search of the country — as well JJ Farman's range. It was all much too large an area for one man alone to undertake the job.

Or, he could ride south to King's Crossing, enlist the help of the town marshal, even hire on some of the loafers always to be found hanging around the saloons . . . That would take time — days, and if Kurt Casey and his bunch had the herd on the move they could get well out of the country before he could return.

The idea didn't appeal to him, anyway. It would be admitting defeat — and it was something he should do on his own. He had gotten himself and the cattle entrusted to him by others, along with his own, into the situation, it was only right and proper he straighten it all out on his own. A man skinned his own snakes, and when he walked into a den of rattlers he shouldn't expect other men to bail him out.

Touching the black with his spurs, he rode back toward the river. He was beginning to feel hunger now, realized that it had been twenty-four hours since he had eaten. Weariness, too, was riding him heavily, but he brushed both from his thoughts; there was no time for food or rest.

Dust, well to the east, claimed his eye just as he reached the Satanta, and he paused, gave it consideration. It was somewhat distant, and it wasn't conceivable that the raiders could have driven the herd so far, but he felt he couldn't afford to ignore the possibility. There had been several hours yet remaining in the day when the herd reached the river; Casey and his crew may have made good use of them. Those minutes, plus the time that had elapsed since daybreak may have afforded enough hours to permit the coverage of the intervening miles.

He spurred the lagging black to a lope, pointed for the dust roil, bringing it into sight a time later. He halted almost immediately, disappointment again filling him. It was a large herd — several thousand steers — moving in from the east. There wasn't a chance that his cattle could be mixed in with them. Disgusted, he came about and returned to the Satanta, reaching the stream well after the noon hour.

Hunger was now an insistent clamoring within him, a companion to the sullen ache in his head, and he realized he would be forced to do something about it. He remembered then the scattered items near the burned chuck wagon, and rode to it, began to pick through the undamaged articles.

He found several tins of peaches, a can half-filled with left-over biscuits that were hard as building bricks, and nothing else of use. But it was something and he sat down at once, cut open two of the cans with his knife and gorged himself on the pickled fruit and crushed hardtack.

Coffee would have been a more than welcome find, but a renewed search failed to turn up the bag he had noticed Milt Fresno kept his stock in, and he guessed it had gone up in the flames along with all the other supplies.

It didn't really matter. He was grateful for what he was able to salvage, and feeling much improved almost immediately, he remounted the black, settling himself gingerly on the horse's broad back in deference to the soreness the lack of a saddle was developing, and once more returned to the river. If he was to find the answer to the puzzle that faced him, it was only logical to believe he'd find it there.

10

Sprawled in the shade along the riverbank, Dave Bradford mulled over his problem. Regardless of how matters appeared, one thing was certain — a herd of cattle simply could not vanish; they had to be around somewhere.

He wrestled with his thoughts, going over the incidents that led up to and followed the stampede as he struggled to find a clue that would shed some light on the mystery. Tired, he dozed off periodically, but always awoke after each short nap with the puzzle foremost in his mind.

Sundown came with a blaze of yellows and golds filling the western sky and bringing relief from the unrelenting heat. He roused, still irritable and impatient with himself because of his failure to find any answers, and then as full darkness spread across Texas Flat, a thought came to him. Mounting the black, he crossed again to the hill near the river from which he had taken earlier observations and once more climbed to its summit . . . Maybe — this time —

A surge of grim satisfaction rolled through him as he leveled his attention to the long plain in the west. A campfire winked in the night. It was somewhat to the north but much too far below to mark the Farman herd he had observed that morning. This was a different camp.

Conviction now building within him, he came off the hill and pointed the black for the distant glow. It dropped from view at once, indicating that it lay in a swale or perhaps a deep arroyo and was considerably below the general ground level.

Five miles or so later he drew in behind a clump of junipers and halted. The smell of wood smoke and singed hair was on the warm, still air, and a faint glare was pocketed near a slope beyond a line of small hillocks just ahead. The dull clink of metal reached his ears. Suddenly tense, he dropped from the gelding, anchored him to one of the shrubs and made his way forward.

He reached the knolls, and on hands and knees, worked to the top. He pulled up short, surprise running through him. It was one of Farman's line camps — a shack, two or three corrals, and a sink in which water stood. He had found the herd.

Going full length onto the stubby grass, he brushed off his hat, stared down into the basin. The old brindle steer that had led the cattle for him, was directly in front of him, a rope snubbing him closely to a corral post. A large part of the herd was in one of the corrals, the remainder, in an adjoining enclosure, were being pulled down, their brands altered and then added to those already wearing a doctored mark.

Nine men were engaged in the operation. Five worked with curved running irons while the others systematically strong armed the waiting steers into position for the blotting. Less than a dozen of the animals were yet to be worked over which meant the raiders had likely been at the job all day.

Curbing an urge to move in, gun blasting, Dave lay back. The mystery of his disappearing herd was now solved. Instead of moving on with the steers, as he had assumed the rustlers would do, they had instead doubled back, probably driving the cattle over the same trail and tracks the animals had made on their approach to the river. Then, at the proper point, they had swung north to the line camp where the brand changing was begun.

He wondered if Farman knew that such

was taking place on his range — a clear act of rustling — decided that he probably did not. The rancher, for all his shortcomings, would not stoop to rustling. Undoubtedly he gave the order to stop any herd crossing Texas Flat and simply left it up to the men involved to do as they saw fit with the cattle . . . But that didn't matter; JJ Farman was still at the bottom of it.

Turning back, Bradford looked again to the camp. Only five more steers remained to be handled. It was too far and the light was not strong enough to tell what changes were being made on his mark, and those of the other Cebolla Basin ranchers — but it would be something for which the outlaws could supply a bill of sale.

His horses were there, too, he saw. The remuda had been driven into the smallest corral while the mounts being used by the rustlers were drawn up to a hitchrack at the side of the shack. He spotted his own sorrel there, along with the horses that Claude Jackson and Earl Ruskin had been riding. Since he did not see the white or the bay that his two other punchers had been using, he guessed he was correct in assuming they had fled the country rather than face the guns of the raiders.

He fell to singling out the rustlers,

studying them as best he could in the pale glare. None appeared familiar although he was certain all were J-Bar-J riders. He did not see either Casey or Earl Macklin, supposed they had returned to the ranch, leaving their friends to do the branding.

Later, either when the herd was again being moved out, or possibly not until it reached the point where a sale could be made, would they show up. It was certain the two men would not risk losing a share of the cash received for the herd by leaving it to their friends — who just might decide to split the proceeds nine instead of eleven ways, and keep going.

The drive would probably begin that next morning, and chances were good the herd would be taken on to Wichita since the rustlers would have no fear of being caught. All those who had been with the cattle were either dead or had left the country entirely, and thus there would be no one to call their hand and accuse them of stealing the herd.

Bradford's mouth pulled down into a hard, crooked grin. They had a surprise coming; he was a long way from being dead — and they sure as hell weren't going to get away with his cattle!

He considered that thoughtfully. Even if

he was able to drive off the raiders and recover the steers, it would be impossible to
handle them alone. He reckoned he could
head back to the Cebolla Basin, or possibly
to King's Crossing, hire punchers as he
had previously thought, but the rustlers
would be out of the line camp and well on
their way to the railhead by the time he
could do that, and the opportunity for re-
covering the beef immediately would have
passed and become more difficult . . . And
he certainly couldn't leave the cattle to run
free while he was gone.

He was thinking foolish, anyway, he decided. Broaching nine men, all hard-case
outlaws — killers — by himself would be
quite a chore. He might cut down three or
four of them but the odds would be too
great and in the end, he'd lose.

Then what? The last thing he intended
to do was just turn around, ride back to
the Cebolla Basin and tell the men who
had placed their faith in him that he'd lost
their cattle and there would be no badly
needed cash for them.

Nor was he going to admit to JJ Farman
that he had failed, that Texas Flat was the
big rancher's exclusive property after all.
He had to come up with something — a
plan that would permit him to recover the

herd and complete the drive.

Once more he settled back to stare up into the star-filled sky. What was to be done, would be done by him alone . . . A big job — get back the cattle and get it to market.

Alone? Why not let the rustlers do it for him?

The thought brought him upright. Why not? Casey and Macklin and their partners thought him dead and feared interference from no one. Let them go ahead, make the drive to Wichita or wherever they were planning to make the sale — and be there to collect.

That was the answer. There were more than enough riders in the party to move the cattle. He could just follow along, keep pace while all the while maintaining a watch over his herd. They would be doing all of the hard work, and in the end he would get the money and at the same time, he'd square up for Milt Fresno and the rest of his crew. When he had completed that little chore, he'd let the law take over.

Bradford smiled in satisfaction. It was a simple plan, and it would work. He glanced again into the hollow. He'd need supplies, however — and a saddle. He'd be damned if he'd ride the black all the way to

Wichita without a hull. He'd just hang around until all was quiet in the camp and then move in, take what he had to have.

11

An owl hooted forlornly into the moonlit night. Dave Bradford stirred restlessly as he stared down into the camp. Only two of the rustlers had rolled up in their blankets and gone to sleep. Those remaining yet sat about the low fire talking, laughing and passing freely a bottle of whiskey back and forth.

Abruptly he came to a decision. He could see no reason to delay any longer. The men were all well on the way to drunken stupors and undoubtedly would shortly fall into a sleep. Rising, he circled the hill, and taking a fair amount of precaution, came into the line camp from the lower end of the corrals.

He halted there, threw his glance toward the glare rising above the shack. He could not see the rustlers from his position but the mutter of their voices and an occasional burst of laughter told him they had not moved. Pressing on, he drew in alongside the pen in which the herd had been placed.

The steers were quiet, satisfied by the hay that had been tossed into the corral and the water, diverted by ditch, from the sink above the shack. Dave looked closely at the brand on the nearest beef. His own Spur mark had been neatly converted by use of a half-circle running iron into a definite wagon wheel.

Curious, he searched about farther. Nate Wheeler's Lazy W was now a Box W; Drury's Circle P had become Circle B. The simple G of Clem Gillis was an O-Bar-O; Calvin Yates's mark had been altered to form a Circle X, and Rodriguez's stock now wore a Double B brand.

It was the work of men adept in the art of altering marks. The cattle, offered for sale with suitable papers, all bearing fictitious names, of course, would be acceptable to any buyer. Apparently Kurt Casey and Macklin had rung in experienced hands to do the job for them.

Dave paused at that thought, wondered again if they were outsiders or some of JJ Farman's regular hired hands — and guessed they would be. Casey and the still-faced Macklin could hardly have had time to seek help elsewhere . . . One thing sure,

Farman certainly wasn't particular about who he hired to ride for him.

Bradford moved on. The talking at the fire had lowered and the laughing ceased. Either the rest of the men had dropped off to sleep or there was a serious and quiet discussion taking place. Reaching the rear of the shack, Dave hunched low and worked his way along its south wall to the front. The rustlers were immediately in front of the small structure, less than a dozen strides distant.

"Still figure we'd be smart to bury them," one of the men was saying. "Somebody just might come along, find them laying there."

"Won't be nothing to find — come dark tomorrow," the puncher next to him countered. "Buzzards and coyotes'll have them all took care of."

"Maybe . . . I didn't see no buzzards hanging around today. Looked three, four times."

"Just hadn't spotted the bodies —"

"Not the damn buzzards! They should've been around right after daylight. They can smell something dead for forty miles!"

"Well, they'll be there tomorrow, you can bet on that," a man sitting opposite the first two said. "Digging holes for them stiffs'd be a lot of work for nothing."

"Just the way I see it," another rustler put in. "And my hands just plain won't fit no shovel handle."

"What did Casey say about it, Kendall? He tell you to bury them?"

Kendall, a broad-faced man with thick shoulders, shook his head, took a pull on the bottle.

The man who had asked the question bobbed his head. "Reckon that settles it then. He didn't figure it was needful so there ain't no sense in us worrying about it. It's his show, him and Macklin's. We ain't supposed to do nothing but take orders."

"And do all the goddam work — and then get the short end of the split."

Kendall lowered the bottle, turned to look at the speaker, a small man with a ragged beard and mustache.

"Well, now, Deke, you just ought've spoke up when we was hatching out this shindig and told Kurt and Guy you didn't like the way they're cutting up the pie! I'm plenty sure they'd've done some changing — just to suit you."

"Wish't I had now," Deke grumbled. "Seems to me we ought to be getting more'n we are. Hell, we done the catching, then worked the whole damned day changing brands, and now we'll be doing the droving — all the way to Wichita. It's a powerful lot of work for what'll be coming to us."

"Better'n regular cowhand wages by a hell of a lot," a voice observed.

"Maybe . . . You ain't having to dodge lead when you're just nursing cows — and if word leaks out that this here Bradford's herd's been rustled —"

"Leak out — how?" Kendall asked patiently. "Who'll ever know until it's too late?"

"The friends of his back in the Basin could be expecting to hear from him. When they don't, they might come looking —"

"And they won't find nothing."

"Just what I'm yammering about. We'd be smart to see that there ain't no sign of Bradford and them others anywhere. They ought to be buried and that wagon covered over . . . Was a damn fool stunt burning it anyway. We could've used it on the drive."

"Can't deny that," Kendall said, "but you're forgetting one thing, George — there ain't nobody going to come looking for quite a spell — maybe even a month, and by then there won't be no signs of anything."

The men fell silent at that. Dave remained crouched beside the wall, occupied now by his own thoughts. He hoped no burial party would be organized to take care of the bodies of Jackson and Ruskin — and his own. Finding him gone and two graves nearby would immediately tip off the rustlers to the fact that he still lived.

But the question seemed to be settled. He watched as the bottle made a final round, was emptied and tossed off into the brush. Three of the men rose, picked up their blanket rolls and finding suitable spots within the circular glare of the fire, turned in. Another reached for a handful of dry branches, tossed them into the flames.

"Ain't we standing a watch?" he asked, glancing at Kendall.

The heavier man laughed. "For what — spooks? Ain't nothing to be looking out for — and we got the herd all penned up tight."

"Was just asking," the puncher said, and selecting a blanket, lay down with the others.

The idea of moving in, having it out with the rustlers again, occurred to Dave Bradford. It would be easy. All were clustered around the fire, some now sound asleep —

and if any offered resistance, use his gun on them — shoot them down as they had Jackson and Milt Fresno and Earl Ruskin. Revenge would be a sweet experience.

But what then of the herd? He couldn't get it to Wichita alone, and spending days rounding up help wasn't feasible. And if he merely captured the outlaws with the thought of forcing them to work as drovers for him, he'd be inviting trouble — possibly death. Such an arrangement would mean constant vigilance day and night, knowing that every man in the party would be waiting for the opportunity to catch him off guard and kill him . . . No, best to stick to his original scheme — let the rustlers, unwittingly, work for him.

"Well, I reckon I'll be getting me some shut-eye, too."

Dave watched the seventh member of the raiders stretch out by the fire and draw his blanket around himself . . . Two yet remaining — Kendall who appeared to be more or less in charge and the older man, George, who had felt all evidence of the raid should be removed.

"You think maybe Deke was right?" the latter said, poking at the fire.

Kendall did not look up. "About what?"

"Saying that we was getting the short end of this here deal. Just been setting here doing some figuring. Way it works out we'll be drawing about five hundred bucks a piece while Kurt and Macklin'll be raking in at least five thousand betwixt them."

Kendall drew out his cigarette makings, rolled himself a smoke in silence. "Guess it ain't exactly no even split," he said finally. "But I ain't about to jump in the middle of them two over it."

"No, but if we maybe was to sort of talk to them, point it out —"

Kendall hung the slim cylinder of tobacco from a corner of his mouth, reached into the fire for a burning brand. Holding it to the cigarette, he sucked it into life, exhaled a cloud of smoke.

"Maybe," he said, tossing the twig back into the flames. "I ain't promising, but if it comes up right, I'll mention it to them — to Kurt, anyway. Can talk to him easier'n I can that Macklin."

George nodded. "Know what you mean. Them dead fish eyes of his'n sort of raise the hairs on the back of a man's neck . . . Well, I'm turning in . . . Boys'll be right pleased to hear you're going to see about getting them more of a share. Deke ain't the first one to mention it some."

"Let's keep it quiet for a spell," Kendall said, quickly. "Chance to talk to Kurt might not come up. It does, then we'll tell them."

"Sure, whatever you say," George replied, and sought out a place among the others for his bed. "Ain't you getting some sleep? Long day coming up tomorrow."

"Aim to crawl in soon as I finish this smoke."

Dave Bradford pulled back into the deeper shadows along the line shack. He had learned little more than what he had already guessed about the rustler's plans, thus he would make no changes. But he should get the things he would need to see him through to Wichita — a saddle, some food.

He glanced toward the now dwindling fire, frowned. The stock of grub carried by the outlaws was apparently inside the shack. Entering the structure would be pushing his luck too far.

Forget that part of it for the time being. There was a sack of coffee beans and a lard tin in his saddlebags. More than likely he'd find a few strips of jerky in the pouches, also . . . With such he could get by until a settlement was reached. All he need do here was get his saddle.

Moving silently, he turned about and started for the hitchrack where he had seen the sorrel.

12

Bradford gained the rear of the line shack, crossed and halted at its opposite corner. The rack was a half a dozen strides away. At his appearance the animals, still saddled, stirred anxiously. He guessed they had been standing there for the entire day, had not been fed or watered.

His first impulse was to free them, let them fend for themselves. They would quickly find the water filled sink and there was ample grass on the nearby slopes, but in that same moment he knew it would be a mistake. The tie ropes of one or perhaps two of the mounts might come loose, but not all. The rustlers would realize instantly that someone had released them and become suspicious.

Quietly, Dave crossed to the rack and shouldered his way in next to the sorrel. He'd like nothing better than to lead the big red horse off, climb aboard, and ride him for the rest of the long drive to

Wichita. But that, too, could lead to trouble. Someone was certain to miss the sorrel, give rise to those same suspicions. He'd just have to make do with the black, a heavier and much slower horse . . . But he would take the saddle.

Reaching for the cinch strap, he unfolded it, slipped the buckle's tongue. The rest of the horses were shifting about nervously, expecting to be fed and watered, and Bradford was continually being crowded into the red gelding.

The cinch loose, he paused, looked toward the yard, hidden from him by the corner of the shack. The noise being set up by the horses could draw attention from Kendall, the one man still awake. Best he be on his way as soon as possible.

Grabbing the hull by the horn, he pulled it from the sorrel. Forced to make room between the red and the animal standing next in the line, Dave's shoulders thumped into the gelding's neighbor, caused it to shy violently. Chain reaction followed as each horse along the pole bar gave ground.

Quickly Bradford ducked under the rack, and keeping the saddle from dragging, recrossed to the rear of the line shack. He had scarcely reached the blackness spread behind it when boot heels sounded just beyond the corner. Kendall's voice, ragged with disgust, came through the night.

"Still standing there — right where we left them this morning . . . Told that squarehead to shuck their gear and give them feed . . . About as dependable as a two year old . . ."

The rap of heels sounded again. Dave, hunched in the darkness, waited. Kendall was going to do something about the horses — feed them or perhaps turn them loose. He could notice the sorrel's missing saddle.

"Easy — easy . . . Whoa now . . ."

The outlaw's words rumbled quietly in the hush as he worked into the animals. Shortly there was a thud as he pulled off a hull, allowed it to fall. The quick tap of hooves followed as the horse moved away.

Kendal was relieving them of their gear — of their heavy saddles, anyway. Chances were he'd not take off the bridle, but leave the reins dragging so they would not wander far . . . There'd be some raw tempers in the morning when some of the mounts turned up with broken leather. Kendall would likely tell whoever complained that it served them right for neglecting their mounts.

The thump of saddles continued at regular intervals, and then came a longer pause. Dave realized the outlaw leader had come to the sorrel, was probably wondering why the red carried no hull while still wearing his bridle.

The silence continued, and then, finally, another saddle was dropped to the ground. Kendall had found some explanation in his mind, had freed the sorrel and moved on to the next horse. Bradford heaved a soundless sigh. That had been close. The outlaw could have wondered about it, and suspicious, aroused the camp.

He would have been trapped since returning to the hills where he had left the black, entailed crossing a considerable amount of open ground — and in such bright moonlight he most certainly would have been spotted. Dave sighed again, hoped his luck would continue to hold.

A slap echoed hollowly. Kendall had relieved the last horse, had sent him on his way after the others, all probably at the sink slaking their thirst.

Bradford felt his muscles grow taut, his nerves sharpen. The rustler could return to his place by the fire — or he could decide to have a look at the horses in the corral, see if they had been cared for. Best he sit tight, wait and see which way the man went before he made a move. His thoughts came to a stop. The dark shape of the outlaw appeared suddenly at the corner of the shack. He had chosen to make a final check before turning in.

Bradford locked his breath, pressed hard against the wall of the small structure. Little more than an arm's reach away Kendall, a fresh cigarette between his lips, strolled by. He was pointing for the lower corral. Dave calculated the man's intentions. If he circled the pens, his return path would bring him along the rear of the shack — and remaining hidden from him would be an impossibility.

Dave drew his pistol. If Kendall did select that path he'd be forced to use the weapon, making of it a club to knock the outlaw cold. To fire a bullet would bring the others down upon him instantly.

Bludgeoning the rustler would also be a bad mistake, he concluded a bit later. Kendall and the rest of the outlaws would know that at least one of the men they had left for dead on Texas Flat was alive and a threat to their plans. He must think of something else.

Easing away from the wall of the shack, he turned his eyes to the rustler. Kendall had stopped at the corral in which the remuda had been stabled and was evidently looking to see if feed had been tossed into it for their use. Seemingly satisfied, he moved on.

Bradford muttered in relief, and picking up his saddle and blanket, hurriedly crossed to the row of pens, following in the outlaw's footsteps. Kendall intended to circle the corrals, not retrace his path. By taking the same course, actually trailing the man, Dave figured he would go unnoticed — at least he would unless Kendall changed his mind.

Bradford grinned tightly. If it came down to that he'd have no alternative but to use his gun on the man — and risk the consequences.

"Kendall?"

The call, breaking suddenly through the night and coming from the corner of the shack, brought Dave to a frozen halt.

"Here," the outlaw answered. He had hesitated at the corral into which the steers had been gathered.

"What the hell's going on? Them horses —"

"Found them still standing at the rack. Told Andy to look after them. He didn't."

"Might've knowed. He's had his snout hung in a bottle ever since we started . . .

He plain ain't worth a goddam when there's whiskey around."

"Ain't worth much when there ain't," Kendall said drily, moving on. "Have trouble sleeping?"

"Some . . . Reckon it was them horses sucking up water that prodded me out. You just aiming to let them run loose?"

"They won't go far. Left the bridles on."

Kendall passed across the opening that lay between the end corral and the line shack, disappeared from sight. The outlaw who had awakened, made some sort of reply, his words indistinct. A few moments later the glare of the fire brightened and Dave guessed the two men had settled down once more — and that he was in the clear.

Throwing the saddle upon his shoulder, he moved on along the corrals, and keeping them between himself and the fire, continued until he was a safe distance from the camp. Then, cutting left, he angled through the low hills to where he had picketed the black.

Cinching the hull onto the horse's broad back, he mounted and pointed for the river. He'd pick up the drive there in the morning, and from then on he'd not let the rustlers and his misbranded herd out of his sight.

Unknown to Kendall and his partners, he would serve as an outrider, looking after them, seeing to it that no harm came to them or to the cattle they were driving . . . He grinned at the thought — a guardian angel for a bunch of renegades.

13

It was late morning when the herd reached the Satanta River. Bradford, after an early breakfast consisting of coffee and a strip or two of salted, dried beef, had awaited the arrival of the rustlers and the cattle impatiently. Any drive, to his way of thinking, should get underway by sunrise. Kendall and his crew of outlaws had wasted almost a half day.

From a screen of willows and doveweed some distance below, he watched the men haze the stock across the stream, giving them but little time to drink before striking out over the last part of Texas Flat.

It was a ragged drive, one that told Dave instantly of the men's inexperience. Small jags of cattle continually wandered off to form separate herds. None of the outlaws were riding drag, apparently having no stomach for the dust that rolled along in the cattle's wake. Many steers lagged behind, became stragglers that had to be driven to catch up. Had the country been one gashed with arroyos and brushy washes, there undoubtedly would have been many losses.

Dave watched from the distance, taking care to remain unnoticed. A position well to the rear seemed to be the safest as the pall lifted by the herd moving now into more dry and less grassy country, gradually increased in density until it became a thick curtain.

Late in the afternoon the herd settled down into a more controlled pattern of motion and Bradford, getting a glimpse of the front line from the edge of a broad swale, spotted a single steer in the lead. The old brindle had taken over command again.

He wondered then where the red-eyed old longhorn had been during the early part of the day, concluded the rustlers, not understanding the reason for his attempts to forge ahead to his customary position, had kept him back in the body of the herd.

The drive should go better now, he thought, glancing toward the lowering sun. Ruling out possible trouble such as a bad storm and a resulting stampede, Kendall and his crew should have few problems getting the herd to Wichita. He did wish, however, that at least two riders would be assigned to the rear of the march; sooner or later there would be some stragglers lost.

The outlaws halted early, bedding the stock in a fairly deep swale that Dave had to admit was an excellent choice. No water was available but grass was plentiful, if dry, and the steers settled in for the night calmly enough.

Bradford made his camp a mile downwind, building a fire against a low butte to trap the glare. He dined on coffee and more of the jerky, and now in possession of his saddle with its blanket roll snugged against the cantle, he was able to spend a more comfortable night.

The rustlers were again late in getting the cattle moving that next day. It was still hours ahead of the schedule they had followed on the previous one, and he took some consolation from that.

The herd should make good time. The sky had begun to fill with clouds shortly after sunrise, turning the air cool, and by noon the promise of rain hung over the land. Not long after the promise became a definite threat. Lightning ripped the heavy overcast and deep-throated thunder rolled ominously. Dave could sense the nervousness that would be spreading through the cattle and swore irritably at the turn of luck that would visit a wild storm upon the country at that particular time when the herd, in the hands of a crew who knew little of trail driving, was on the trail.

At the first spatter of hard drops, he pulled his slicker free of the strings that secured it to the saddle, and drew it on. Because of the darkness settling over the flat as the storm closed in, he could not see whether the outlaws had come equipped for such occasions or not. If they lacked the essential gear their job of looking after the steers would be doubly difficult and thoroughly disagreeable.

Abruptly the rain increased, turned from a hasty shower of large drops to a thrashing downpour. The crackle of lightning and booming of thunder heightened. Now worried, Dave Bradford began to press in nearer to the herd, keeping the black below the ridges and in the swales to avoid being seen.

The cattle came into view as he rounded one of the larger knolls. They had evidently halted of their own accord, were huddled in a fairly tight bunch, heads down, wet hides glistening sleekly in the vivid flashes of lightning. He located the outlaws after some difficulty. They had pulled into a cluster of junipers, were endeavoring futilely to find shelter from the driving rain under the thin branches of the scrubby trees. Only three of the party wore slickers.

The storm raged on with no let-up. Bradford, taking no chances, kept well in the clear of Kendall and his men, his mind eased somewhat by the knowledge that so far the cracking and rumbling seemed not to disturb the cattle to any extent.

And then suddenly that all changed. A brilliant streak broke the heavens wide open. A ball of fire struck the ground, exploded, sent fragments of fire rolling to all directions as the air rocked with cannon-like sound and the heavy downpour changed to a descending torrent.

Above the roaring of the storm a new and different thunder became audible — a dull rumbling that brought Dave Bradford's heart into his throat. The cattle were running . . . Stampede!

Rising in his stirrups, he tried to pierce the murky curtain of rain. The flat that only moments before had been covered by the dark mass of the herd, was emptying rapidly. Somewhere on the far side a gunshot echoed faintly, and he knew by it that the rustlers were aware of the break, were evidently trying to do something about it,

He spurred the reluctant black to a rise immediately ahead, crossing a narrow wash that was beginning to flow with thick, roily water. Lightning filled the sky again. He saw the herd. It was moving straight away, pointing, fortunately in the direction of the drive . . . But there would be disaster if the land proved to be broken, laced with arroyos and buttes, even though low in height.

Blindly running steers would stumble and fall in such hazards. Those behind them would continue to come and such a pile-up could wipe out an entire herd.

More gunshots flatted through the howling of the storm. Dave, anxious, continued his paralleling course below the onrushing steers. He saw nothing of the rustlers who should be riding with the herd, forming a half circle around it, holding it on trail and in as tight a formation as possible to prevent scattering.

He swore, considering that. Likely the men were too interested in looking out for themselves to take any precautions concerning the cattle. Frowning, he pulled in the black, brushed at his eyes in order to see better. A wedge of the racing, black mass, was slicing away, veering to the south . . . The herd was splitting.

Grim, he wheeled the gelding sharp right, and ignoring the possibility of encountering any of the outlaws, rode hard to get ahead of the splinter herd. The black was a team horse unaccustomed to saddle work and he reacted slowly, but Dave roweled him out to where he was abreast the cattle. Then, pulling off his slicker, he cut straight for the foremost steer and began to wave the water polished poncho over his head.

The leaders, eyes rolling white in the wet, spooky gloom, shied at once, began to turn away. The remainder, a hundred animals or so, followed at once. Shortly the entire bunch was racing back in the direction of the main body.

Bradford halted, fearing to get any closer. He had seen none of Kendall's party but knew that such was no assurance that they had not caught sight of him. If so, it would have been at a distance, and with vision limited by the hammering rain, it was more than possible he would have been taken for one of the others. He wouldn't crowd his luck farther, however. Someone might move in for a better look.

He eased away, maintaining again the

paralleling path he had pursued. Only now and then when a broad flash of lightning came did he get a glimpse of the cattle — still running but now at slower pace. The rain showed no indication of slackening and the arroyos and washes were now carrying full quotas of rushing, silt laden water to be deposited in the low-lying sinks farther on.

Finally the downpour began to fade. A break in the dark, hanging clouds appeared and a patch of blue sky, small at first, widened steadily.

Dave dropped farther back as the land grew lighter, and by the time the falling drops had ceased entirely, he had resumed his customary position well away from the outlaws and the cattle, now halted in a small valley that lay between two fairly high hills. The storm was over and there should be no more danger. Dave could only hope that losses had not been too great.

14

Near midnight a second rain began to fall but it was of short duration and accompanied by only a small amount of thunder and lightning. Bradford, rolled in his blanket in the comparative dryness beneath a sage clump, roused at the touch of the first drop and prepared to ride. The cattle, rested now, could become excited and stampede again.

But the storm passed over swiftly and Dave lay back under the dripping branches to catch a few more hours of sleep.

He was up long before the sun, and scrounging around under the brush clumps, managed to scrape together enough dry wood for a low fire. He made coffee and ate the last of the jerky. His supply of coffee beans was almost gone, too, only enough remaining for one more camp.

He would be forced to ride ahead, find a ranch or a town where he could buy a stock of food, he realized. The thought was a pleasant one. He was thoroughly sick of living on salt-larded beef that was closely akin to rawhide.

Finished with his meal, he saddled the black and rode east. The herd was somewhere to his left, and if the outlaws ran true to form, they would not have the cattle moving for another hour or two. It could even be later than that if there had been some particular difficulty where the steers were concerned.

One thing that undoubtedly would slow the drive down considerably was the lack of spare horses. The rustlers had not bothered to bring along the remuda they had acquired when taking over the herd, but were relying upon the ones they had been riding.

After the stampede during which those horses were called upon to work exceptionally hard even though they had already put in a long day, all would be in poor condition to continue the drive. Thinking back to the line camp and the manner in which the men had cared for their mounts, Dave guessed such would have little bearing on the outlaws' plans; they would push their horses regardless of condition and if any broke down they would simply find replacements somewhere.

Sometime later he caught sight of the

herd, much farther to the north than he had expected. It was a dark wedge crawling slowly up a slope, seemingly setting its own pace. The outlaws had the cattle moving again, if at a desultory speed.

Turning back, he rode due north until he was behind the herd, and then swung west over the tracks they had left in the soft, wet soil.

He reached the point where the cattle had bedded down, continued on. At a narrow but deep wash he saw the first of the casualties — two steers. A short distance farther along he came upon two more. They were in the open and on level ground. Evidently they had simply slipped on the rain-slicked grass, fallen and been trampled by the wall of cattle that had swept over them.

Dave found three additional beeves, all in a fairly wide arroyo that looked as if it had carried a strong body of run-off water during the storm. Only a small trickle flowed along its course now, and by dark he knew all traces of the muddy torrent that had rushed down its graveled floor would have been erased by the hot sun.

Seven steers . . . That was bad — a hard loss to take, but he knew it could have been much worse. He reckoned he couldn't blame Kendall and the other out-laws too much for it; even had he been there with his own crew the results would likely have been the same. There was little any man, experienced or not, could do when a herd became frightened and set it-self to a blind, wild run in a bad storm.

But he felt the loss keenly, nevertheless, and turning, he followed his own trail back over Texas Flat until he saw the herd in the distance.

Bradford pulled up at once. The cattle were still moving slowly and he must again use care and not get too close. There was greater danger now of being seen since the rain had converted what loose dust there was into soft mud and he no longer had a protective screen to remain behind.

Dismounting, Dave let his eyes sweep the country. It was fresh and green casted after the thorough washing down it had sustained, and from a distance appeared to be covered with a solid carpet of grass. They should be off Texas Flat by now, he reasoned, and not too far from the Wichita Trail — which also could mean they would soon come to a settlement.

He gave that thought. The sight of the dead steers had set up a disturbing worry within him, one he knew would not be satisfied until he again had a crew of his own and was heading up the drive as he had been at the start.

If the town was one of any size he could, perhaps, hire on punchers, recover his cattle and resume command. It would mean a showdown with the rustlers but he'd have the law on his side and there shouldn't be too much difficulty involved. Letting Kendall and his partners take the cattle on in to Wichita was fine — if there was no other answer, but he'd much prefer to do it himself.

He'd look into it, he decided, going back to the saddle and riding on. As soon as he was certain they were approaching a settlement, he'd circle wide and get there well ahead of the outlaws. If things went right, it just could be he'd have everything ready and jail cells awaiting the men Kurt Casey and Guy Macklin had hired to raid his drive.

The day wore on with the cattle moving agonizingly slow. It would have been an ideal time to force the pace, the ground being moist, even wet in places, and the air cool despite a strong sun. But the outlaws were not taking advantage of it, seemingly were satisfied to let the herd amble along aimlessly. They were watching the stragglers and the ones that attempted to cut away from the main body, however, and that was an improvement.

He hoped there would be no more losses, that he had seen the last of such things as stampedes now that they were coming on to the main trail. He could feel more certain of it, though, if it developed that he could hire his own punchers when they reached a settlement. Men hanging around a trail town were usually drovers who could be depended upon to know their business, and with the right hands riding for him, he should be able to make Wichita without losing more beef.

A far-off wisp of smoke spiraling thinly into the still air caught his attention. He halted at once, studied it carefully. It originated in the area along which he guessed the trail ran and could, therefore, be a hoped for town.

Turning his glance to the sun, he gauged its position. The herd would likely reach the settlement by dark, possibly a little before. By horseback he should be able to cover the distance in two hours more or less.

He swung his attention to the herd, wondering idly if the rustlers had noticed the smoke. If so, they might take it in mind to speed up the herd. Doubtless they were as anxious to reach a town as was he except theirs would be for different reasons.

Shortly it looked to him as if the cattle had picked up the pace somewhat and were veering more to the north instead of following a direct eastward line. It could only mean the outlaws had spotted the smoke column and were now making an effort to reach its source as soon as possible.

At once Bradford swung back, and dropping behind a rise that shut him off from view of the men, spurred the black into a steady lope.

He reached the flat upon which the settlement had been built well ahead of the outlaws, as he had anticipated, and drew to a halt in the trees along its edge. Disappointment slogged through him.

It was far from a town — one two-storied house half of which was devoted to a general store, the other to a saloon. In the rear of the structure was a line of squatting huts connected by a single roof; quarters for the women he could see lounging on the saloon's gallery and under the overhang fronting their cribs.

Farther on he could see a large, brush-fence corral where herds could be penned while the drovers took a break from the trail and laid over for a night of bawdy recreation . . . It was only a trail stop — a way station.

Dave swore deeply. He'd get no help there. Turning, he rode back into the grove to await the arrival of the rustlers and his herd.

15

It was full dark by the time the cattle were in the improvised corral provided for the convenience of customers and the outlaws had retired to the murky interior of the saloon.

A single bracket lamp burned on the porch of the bulky structure, spreading a dim half-circle of yellow light on the plank flooring. Inside the illumination appeared to be only a little better, and sitting his saddle on the black in the deep shadows of the trees across the clearing, Dave could make out only the vague figures of the rustlers lined up at the bar while the slatternly women he had noticed earlier moved languidly among them.

He turned his attention to the other half of the building where shelves and counters of food stuff, dry goods and similar general merchandise were visible through the dust-filmed windows. Not wishing to appear conspicuous, he had purposely delayed until Kendall and his outlaw crew had arrived before showing himself. He should now be able to pass as one of the party with no difficulty and thus draw no undue attention from the storekeeper.

Touching the black with his rowels, Dave crossed to the rack at the store half of the structure and dismounted. Removing his hat he stuffed it into a pocket of his saddlebags, and moving up onto the porch, entered.

He halted at the drygoods counter, eyes running the shelf upon which several broad-brimmed hats were displayed. It had occurred to him, as he waited, that it would be wise to change his appearance as much as possible.

While he did not know any of the men involved in the raid, with the exception of Macklin and Casey, it was likely all could recognize him, if not from incidental meetings in the Basin, from the encounter on Texas Flat. Now, with many days yet ahead of them before Wichita would be reached during which time the possibility of his being seen, at least from a distance, would be much greater, altering his looks was only good, common sense.

The rustle of cloth brought him about. A woman in her late twenties or early thirties, dull hair pulled to a bun on the nape of her neck and wearing a bulky, floor-length dress of some sleazy gray material, regarded him with sullen eyes.

"Like to buy myself a hat," Bradford said, pointing to a black, flat-crowned number on the shelf.

The woman moved in behind the counter, took down the one indicated and wordlessly handed it to him. He tried it on. It was a half size large but since it was far different from the one he had been wearing, he'd make it do.

"How much?"

"Be five dollars."

The cost was high. Generally prices in such places were unusually out of line, however, and he did have the need.

"How about a shirt. Something in flannel — and anything but gray."

Silent, the woman probed through a small stack on the counter and produced a green and a blue. Dave measured the blue against his shoulders. It would serve the purpose.

"Two dollars," the woman said without waiting to be asked.

A burst of laughter came from the adjoining saloon, penetrating the thin wall separating the two establishments as easily as if there had been no partition at all. The woman's lips tightened but she said nothing, merely waited, hands folded in front of her.

"Need some trail grub. Coffee, flour, meat, tinned goods — and the like."

She turned, walked from the drygoods section through the clutter to a back counter. Dave, beginning to pull off his shirt, named the items he desired, and as she went about the business of assembling them, he drew on the new green and blue shirt and set the hat on his head. When she was finished, he had completed the change.

"Be ten dollars for all of it — everything," the woman announced in her wooden way, dumping the supplies into a flour sack. And then, as Bradford looked about questioningly, added, "You want a room, go next door. Buck'll fix you up."

Dave dropped a ten-dollar gold piece on the counter, shook his head. "Was wondering about getting myself a meal."

She picked up the coin, dropped it into a pocket and looked more closely at him. "Ain't you with them others?"

"Rode in with them," he replied offhandedly. "I'm more interested in eating than drinking right now."

She thought for a moment, shrugged.

"Reckon I could fix you up back there," she said, jerking her head at a door in the rear of the building. "Be steak and beans. Coffee . . . Maybe some pie. Cost you another dollar."

Evidently the meal would be served in the family kitchen, which was not connected to the saloon. He'd run no risk encountering the outlaws.

"Be fine. Can I eat now?"

For the first time the woman's expression changed. The ghost of a smile lifted the corners of her lips.

"Might as well," she murmured, and turned to the door.

The kitchen was small, filled with the smells of burned grease, kerosene, and coffee boiled too long. Dave crossed to the far side, sat down at a table placed against an inside wall and settled back, listening to the steady racket and confusion coming from the saloon as the woman went about the chore of preparing the food.

Once the steak was in a pan and frying, she brought a clean plate and wooden-handled knife and fork, set them before him on the worn oilcloth cover.

"You all headed for Wichita?" she asked without looking at him.

Bradford nodded.

She went back to the stove, flipped the slab of meat in the sizzling grease, then opened the warming oven and took out several squares of cornbread. The coffeepot was beginning to pour steam from its spout. Stacking the cornbread on another plate, she put it aside, filled a cup from the pot and handed it to him. Dave could smell its strength as he took it from her, guessed it had been brewed early that morning.

But it tasted good and was just what he needed. He finished off the cup as she placed the meal before him and he immediately put his attention to it. The meat and beans were exactly as he liked them, and cornbread was never better — all of which could have found basis in the fact that he had not partaken of a square meal in days.

Refilling his coffee cup, she sat down at the opposite side of the table. "You wouldn't be looking for traveling company, would you?"

Dave paused, glanced up at the woman's question. She was staring at him earnestly, but a natural aversion to becoming involved in something that was none of his business pushed through him.

"No . . ."

"I see."

A chair crashed against the wall's opposite side. A shout followed and then a man's deep voice growled:

"Watch what you're doing — goddammit!"

"Would only be far as Wichita."

Again Bradford hesitated in his eating, caught up by the desperate note of appeal in her voice.

"You talking about yourself?"

She nodded wearily. "Been wanting to pull out for quite a spell. Made up my mind a few days ago I'd leave first chance I got."

"What about your husband?"

She shook her head. "Buck ain't my husband. He just brought me here about a year ago. Was one of the girls he keeps around for the trail hands. Changed his mind and sort of made me his private woman. Ended up with me running this here store and doing his cooking and cleaning and such . . . Goddam tired of it . . . Tired of him spending his time with them other girls and not paying no mind to me."

She arose impulsively, stood before him. Squaring her shoulders she ran her hands down her sides and over her hips.

"I ain't so bad looking, am I?" she asked

childishly. "I get on a proper dress and fix up my hair and face a bit, I'm just as pretty as them others!"

Dave considered her for several moments. "Bet you are — and maybe that's what you ought to do — pretty yourself up like you said. Then this Buck'll probably pay plenty of attention to you . . . What's your name?"

"Annie Gilmore," the woman said, pursing her lips. "You really think maybe that'd happen — that Buck would pay me some mind was I to do that?"

"He'd be loco if he didn't. Why don't you pick yourself a fine dress from the stock in the store —"

Alarm filled her eyes. "He'd beat hell out of me —"

"Not if I bought the dress, gave it to you."

Annie smiled brightly. "Say, that would sure shake him up some — another man buying me some clothes!" She paused, stared at him. "Would you do that for sure, mister?"

Bradford drained his coffee cup. It was a quick and easy way out of being saddled with company he could not afford to have along.

"Be my pleasure. I figure Buck needs his

eyes opened some. How much will a dress cost?"

"Got one in there for five dollars I can fix up real nice."

"Good," Bradford said, rising. Reaching into a pocket he drew out the necessary amount for it and the meal.

She pushed one of the silver dollars back to him. "Supper ain't going to cost you nothing," she said, adding the rest of the coins to the gold piece. "I'm going to get busy right now, fixing myself up . . . Sure am obliged to you . . . Folks always said I was a real looker. I get ready I'll come in there and show you."

"I'll be waiting," Dave said.

"Won't take me more'n a hour or two. When I'm done I aim to just go sailing right in there, right in front of God and everybody, let them all pop out their eyes . . . Bet that Buck won't ever take another look at that Minnie Jo he brung in here from Fort Worth, once he sees me!"

Bradford moved toward the door. "I'm betting he won't either," he agreed, and returning to the store, picked up his sack of groceries and walked quickly to the rack where his horse waited.

16

Dave Bradford heaved a sigh of relief as he tucked his supply of grub and the shirt he had replaced into his saddlebags. He was glad to get away from Annie Gilmore and her troubles with the man she called Buck, who evidently had taken a shine to one of the new girls he'd imported to work for him. He felt sorry for her but the last thing he wanted to do was get involved in what amounted to a family squabble.

Unhooking his canteen, he poured its remaining contents onto the ground, and stepping to the water trough and pump at the rear of the store, refilled it. The racket within the saloon had increased, and glancing to the rear entrance, Dave had a momentary impulse to slip in, have himself a couple of drinks. He had more than earned them in those past few days, but it would be a foolhardy risk to take and he immediately dropped the thought.

The door opened. One of the rustlers,

singing raucously and accompanied by a woman in a faded red dress, appeared. They paused on the steps, the man swaying dangerously, and then together they descended the short flight and headed unsteadily for the row of cribs farther on.

Bradford remained motionless until they had passed from view, and then again started for his horse. He halted, froze a second time as the door once more swung back. Kendall and the older man called George moved into the open, started down the steps. Halfway Kendall hesitated, looked back into the saloon.

"Where's Deke?"

"He'll be coming," George replied. "What's on your mind?"

A third figure appeared in the doorway, a bottle in hand. "You wanting me?"

"Yeh . . . Got some talking to do."

Bradford, fearing to make any further moves toward the waiting black gelding, hunched behind the horse trough.

"The rest of the boys — you want —" Deke began.

"Forget them," Kendall snapped. "This here's for you and George to hear. Want to talk about the split —"

"Split?" Deke echoed thickly, and came farther onto the landing. "What split? Oh

— you're meaning the share we're getting in Wichita," he added and moved on down the steps.

Kendall, pulling away from the light that spilled through the open doorway, halted, shoulders against the wall of the building and began to roll himself a cigarette. George, followed by Deke drew up before him. He took a swallow of the liquor, handed the bottle to the older man.

"The split — what about it?"

"Been thinking over what you said. Sure don't seem right us getting no more'n we are when we're doing all the work."

"Just what I was telling you," Deke said, bobbing vehemently. "Was exactly what I said."

"Now, I ain't never a body to go double-crossing a man," Kendall continued, "especially the likes of Kurt Casey and Macklin, but if it could be done and we could get the hell clean out of the country before they knowed about it, I'd sort of go for the idea. Understand what I mean?"

Deke nodded again. George, considerably more sober, was doubtful.

"Don't hardly see how that could be done."

"Wouldn't be too hard. Kurt and Macklin are meeting us in Wichita on the fifteenth. That's the day I said we'd be there — figuring to take it easy like all the way. Now, was we to start pushing them cows hard, we could lop off a couple, maybe even three days and get there ahead of them plenty."

George slapped his hands together. "And make us a deal with some buyer and be long gone by the fifteenth! By damn, it'll be easy!"

Crouched in the shadows behind the trough, Dave considered the plan Kendall had advanced. It didn't matter to him when the herd reached Wichita, he would be the one to collect for the sale, anyway . . . But he had looked forward to the reckoning with Macklin and Kurt Casey. That could come later, at another time and place.

There was one drawback to the rustlers' idea; in their anxiety to reach the railhead well before the fifteenth of the month, they might drive the cattle so hard that several would be sacrificed in the interest of speed, and he had already sustained all the losses he cared to take.

"Be hanging an ax over our heads," Kendall pointed out. "Don't forget that. Kurt and Macklin'll be looking for us from then on, and was any of us to ever meet up with either one of them, it'll be a case of getting in the first shot — or dying."

"I ain't no great shakes on fast drawing," Deke said in a plaintive voice. "Was they to collar me —"

"Thing for you to do is practice running," George cut in drily, and then added, facing Kendall, "How about the rest of the boys? You counting them in on it?"

"Have to. Need them to help get them cows in to Wichita."

"Reckon so, but I was thinking we could go right ahead, make the deal, then pay them what they're figuring on getting — five hundred apiece."

Kendall puffed slowly on his smoke. Finally, "Would sure make it a fat cut for us, doing it that way. Think it'd work?"

"Why wouldn't it? We just don't tell them no different and they won't know no different — leastwise, not until Kurt and Macklin show up, and we'll be a far piece aways by then."

"Man could cover a lot of ground in three days hard riding," Kendall admitted. "Could dang near be in Mexico, was he to try."

"Good place to head for . . . Could light out together, all three of us. Would be safer was we to sort of stay in a bunch."

Kendall nodded, flipped his dead cigarette into the yard. He glanced at Deke, now numbed by the quantity of liquor he had drunk and only barely aware of what was taking place.

"Wish't now we'd a left him out of it. You figure he can keep his mouth shut?"

George shrugged. "He'll be all right once he sobers up. Likes money too much to go spoiling anything."

"I don't know . . . Just ain't so sure about him."

"Easy took care of," George said. "I'll put him to bed, let him sleep off that whiskey. When he wakes up I'll tell him again what we're doing."

"I know what we're doing," Deke declared belligerently. "We're double-crossing Kurt and Guy so's we can take all the money."

Kendall and George exchanged glances. Deke had not been as far gone as he had pretended.

"And what're you meaning — that I'm easy took care of?"

George laughed, a hasty sound. "Why, that you'd be reasonable and go on to bed — that's all."

"Sure," Kendall added. "You've had more'n your share of that redeye and we

140

don't want nothing to happen that might slanchways our scheme. Best thing for you to do is turn in right now."

"Not yet. Got my eye on that little black-haired Mex gal —"

"Not tonight. We pull off this deal we've cooked up and you can have yourself a half a dozen like her."

Deke wagged his head stubbornly, glanced at the whiskey bottle in his hand, and seeing that it was empty, hurled it off into the weeds behind the cribs. "It ain't later I'm wanting her — it's now!"

George studied the puncher thoughtfully. After a moment he swung his attention to Kendall.

"Think it'd hurt?"

Kendall pulled away from the wall of the building. "Maybe not — but we sure got a lot to lose. Expect you ought to bed him down whether he likes it or not."

Deke took a step toward the man, almost fell, caught at George to save himself. He was only a breath away from passing out.

"I ain't going to no bed — not yet . . . Not until I get me that little Mex," he stated thickly.

"Could get him set, then take her to him," George said.

"And have him running off at the mouth

to her about what we're doing? No, put him to bed and forget her."

"Supposing he won't stay put?"

Kendall shrugged. "Only one thing you can do, and I reckon you know what that is. Got to protect our interests — savvy?"

"Sure do," George replied, and taking Deke's arm, turned him about and headed for the steps. "Come on, pardner —"

Deke drew back, endeavored to pull away. "I'm waiting for that little Mex — I keep telling you —"

"Know that," George said placatingly. "Aim to fetch her for you . . . But first off, we got to find you a bed."

Satisfied Deke allowed George to take a firm grip on his arm and steer him toward the door. Kendall remained motionless, staring after the two men until they had disappeared into the building, and then taking out his sack of tobacco and fold of papers, rolled himself another cigarette. A match flared in his cupped hands, briefly lighting the planes of his face as he held it to the tip of his smoke, puffed it into a red coal. After that he dropped the match to the ground and moved on slowly in the direction of the cribs.

Dave waited until the outlaw had rounded the corner of the row, and came to an upright position. He couldn't see that the new plan would hurt him in any way; it would merely shorten the length of the drive. The one danger it might present was the possible loss of steers if the men pushed the herd too hard — and he might be able to prevent that.

Wheeling, he returned to the black, and mounting, rode toward the brush corral where the cattle had been bedded down. He'd see to it that they were all right, then drop back into the trees a safe distance and wait out sunrise.

17

True to plan the rustlers were up early and had the herd on the trail by daybreak. Dave, hidden in the grove east of the way stop, watched the cattle pour through the gate of the corral in which they had spent the night, and flow out in a brown and white rectangle onto the level ground.

They had bedded well and were in good condition to travel. A fairly good stream cut through the enclosure, affording them ample water, and while previous herds had cropped the grass to near ground, there was still enough available to satisfy their needs.

Several of Buck's women stood on the saloon waving their farewells to the riders and once Dave saw Annie Gilmore moved up close to the window of the store and stare thoughtfully after the departing out-laws.

He wondered how her plan to reattract Buck to her charms had turned out; successfully, he hoped, and again breathed a sigh at his good fortune in dissuading her from leaving the man and becoming a part of his problems.

He had plenty of those, he thought, eyes again on the herd now directly opposite his place of concealment. He would as soon the rustlers had stuck to their original plan, the one laid down by Casey and Macklin; it meant less complication. But Kendall and his two partners were taking it upon themselves to rustle the herd from the rustlers and claim the greater share of the profits for themselves — so it was them with whom he now must deal.

His only present worry was a need to keep losses at a minimum. A drive expected to lose a few, and so far they had actually been more fortunate than usual, probably because of the more than average number of riders moving the herd. But a forced drive such as the outlaws were undertaking would increase the probability of loss.

Bradford rubbed at the stubble sprouting from his chin. He had counted only eight men. Immediately the question of identity came to him. Who was missing? Was it Deke? He spurred the black to the edge of the grove, sought to get a closer look at each of the men.

A faint dust haze was beginning to hang in the cool air and visibility wasn't too good. Also, several of the riders, once the cattle were on the way, had promptly dropped off to sleep in the saddle, heads hung forward, chins sunk into their chests while they rocked back and forth to the rhythm of their horses.

He was certain it was Deke, and the final words that Kendall had spoken to George that previous night came to mind. Evidently Deke had gotten out of hand and George had silenced him once and for all.

No pity stirred through Dave Bradford at the realization of the fate that had overtaken the man. It meant, simply, that he would have one less rustler to deal with when the time came, and that was good. Deke deserved no consideration, as far as he was concerned; he had been a part of the murders of Claude Jackson, and Ruskin and Milt Fresno. He was getting his due — from his own kind, oddly enough.

What would Kendall and George tell the others? How would they explain the absence of the missing outlaw to his friends? Since they were cutting them out of the plan to double-cross Casey and Macklin, they could not give the real reason. It would have to be for some trumped up cause — a drunken brawl, or perhaps they would blame it on one of Buck's women . . . Whatever it was had evidently satisfied the men since there was no sign of trouble.

The herd moved out of sight, following a broad trail that lifted and fell along the rolling land. They were traveling at a good pace, indicative of Kendall's determination to reach Wichita well before the two gunmen, and at such rate if no unexpected delays were encountered, they would do so easily.

Roweling the black, Bradford began to follow, keeping even with the tail of the herd but staying well within the band of trees that paralleled their course. If such cover would continue he'd find it simple to maintain his surveillance of the cattle and never be noticed by the rustlers. It was ideal; he was near enough to see all that transpired yet was completely shut off from the eyes of the riders . . . It was too good to last, he was sure.

Noon came and with it a strong build up of the day's heat. The cattle began to slow but the outlaws refused to permit it and kept after them relentlessly. Kendall undoubtedly now regretted his decision to bring no remuda for it was clear the horses they were riding would soon break down under such hard work.

Two passers-by caught up with the drive around the middle of the afternoon, slowed to ride along with it and talk with Kendall and some of the others for a few miles, and then continued on their way. Strangers enroute to Wichita, Dave guessed, or perhaps some more distant point; at any rate they were in too much of a hurry to tarry with the slower traveling herd even though the cattle were making far better than average time.

By late afternoon, with the heat lying solid over the great, rolling plains across which they were moving, the steers began to show signs of tiring. Again Kendall and his crew worked at keeping them on the march, weaving back and forth on foam-flecked horses, shouting, swinging their ropes and occasionally shooting their guns while their own clothing became dark with sweat.

It was much different when the stakes involved were their own, Bradford thought as he watched the men at their labor. Hiring drovers to push a herd that hard would be next to impossible; when it was to their own advantage, it became a different matter.

Around dusk they dropped off a slight rise and dipped into a small valley where a stream laid a bright slash along its floor. It was an ideal spot for a night camp, and evidence indicated that it had been used as such by many previous herds.

But Kendall and his riders decreed otherwise. There were still a good two hours of daylight remaining, and the rustler leader permitted the steers to pause only long enough for a drink and then with gunshots, and more yells and flailing ropes, forced them away from the creek and on down the trail.

It was a difficult job. The steers were stubborn, the riders and horses both tired, but the men prevailed and the herd ambled on until at last closing darkness brought a halt in another short valley. There was no water available but the slopes had a fair stand of grass, and since the cattle had watered Dave knew they would not suffer from thirst.

All became quiet at once. The steers, tired from the long hard day, settled down quickly. And as fast, the outlaws, after seeing to their weary mounts for a change, gathered around a small cook fire, blankets already spread and waiting for them as soon as the meal was over.

Bradford waited until most of the men had turned in, then worked his way out of the trees and into the camp, coming up behind the horses where he would not be noticed.

He halted there, picketed the black, and edged in close to the rustlers' horses with the intention of looking them over carefully. Their importance to him now was equaled only by the ability of the outlaws themselves in getting his herd to the railhead.

Saddles and bridles had been removed, he noted with satisfaction, and the animals were tethered by a short rope to a picket line strung between two shrubs. Grain had evidently been purchased from Buck's store at the trail stop, for now a small quantity had been dumped on the ground in front of each horse.

There was no hay about, but the length of the tie ropes would permit grazing to some extent when the grain was gone. No water was to be had but they, too, had satisfied their thirsts at the stream they had crossed earlier.

It was a relief to Bradford; the rustlers were now according their mounts at least token care. The animals would never reach Wichita if the neglect he had witnessed back up the trail continued. Hunching, he began to scoop the scattered grain into piles in front of each horse so that it could more easily be lipped into the mouth. The portions meted out had been small and none of it should be wasted.

Dave paused, drew himself upright. The steady tattoo of a rider coming up the road from the south hung in the warm, night air.

Another pilgrim enroute north — or could it be Deke? Perhaps he was not dead after all, had instead been sent to do an errand or similar chore and was now returning to the drive. The hoofbeats grew louder, and then shortly the rider was moving into the glare of the fire. Dave stared, frowned. It was Annie Gilmore.

18

Kendall and the man squatting beside him rose slowly. Another of the outlaws, already sleeping but disturbed by the hoofbeats entering camp, rolled over and sat up.

The outlaw chief brushed his hat to the back of his head, peered at the girl. "Say — ain't you Buck's woman — the one running the store?"

Annie threw a leg over her saddle, clutched at her skirt and dropped to the ground. "I was," she replied coldly. Glancing around at the blanketed, snoring shapes, she added: "I'm looking for a friend."

The man next to Kendall laughed. "What's the matter? Somebody forget to pay up?"

Annie shook her head. She was wearing a bright yellow dress, Dave noted, and guessed it was the one he had financed for her in the attempt to win back Buck. She had applied rouge and powder to her face and he realized she was a much more attractive woman than a first impression had indicated.

"You mean you're hunting one of my crew?" Kendall asked.

She nodded, drew the light jacket she had pulled on tighter about her body to ward off the chill that was now settling in.

"What's his name?"

"I don't know. Just met him. In the store — last night."

Kendall turned to the rider beside him. "Weren't none of us in that store last night, was there, Joe? Done all our buying early this morning."

Joe bobbed his head. "Near as I recollect, we all hit the saloon, then the shacks." He glanced at Annie. "Reckon you're wrong, lady. Wasn't none of us."

"He came in while all the rest of you was in the saloon. Bought himself a new hat and shirt . . . And some groceries."

Kendall stiffened. For a long minute he was silent, and then: "Why are you hunting this jasper?"

Annie Gilmore looked off into the night. "I'm leaving Buck. Was telling him about it. Sort of figured I'd team up with him — at least 'til we got to Wichita."

"He say for you to do that?"

"Well — no, not exactly."

"What about Buck?"

"He don't give a damn — he's so wrapped up in that there Minnie Jo."

"Minnie Jo —" the rustler near the fire who had been aroused by the woman's arrival, whistled softly. "I can see why. She sure is a looker."

"I was, too — once," Annie said plaintively.

The rustler grinned. "Yes'm — and you still are."

Kendall drew out his cigarette makings, set himself to building a smoke as he eyed the woman.

"You figure you'd know this man was you to see him again?"

"Course I would!"

Bradford swore under his breath. Kendall's suspicions had been stirred into life by Annie's words. The plans he had in mind could suddenly go down a rat hole.

Kendall ducked his head at Joe. "Wake 'em up, let her take a look. I'm real interested in knowing who this bird is she's hunting for."

The rustler moved in among the men stretched out around the fire, kicking each into wakefulness. Muttering and cursing, they sat up. Only George got to his feet.

"What the hell's going on?" he demanded, crossing to where Kendall stood.

"Lady here's looking for a friend."

"In the middle of the goddam night?" one of the rustlers muttered. "For hell sake, I'm —"

"Take a good look at them," Kendall directed, motioning at Annie.

She crossed in front of him, made a tour of the riders, staring down at each intently. When she had completed the circuit, she returned to the rustler.

"He's not one of them."

Kendall swore angrily, hurled his unlit cigarette into the fire. "Just what I was afeared of!"

George rubbed at his jaw, perplexed. "You mind telling me what the hell this is all about?"

"Was a jasper in Buck's store last night, buying himself grub — and a new hat and shirt. Claimed he was one of our bunch. She's looking for him."

"So?"

"Why would he be telling her a yarn like that?"

George thought for a moment. His head came up abruptly. "Yeh — why would he? Something mighty funny here."

"What's this fellow look like?" Kendall

said, turning back to the woman.

Annie hesitated, again lowered her eyes as if realizing she was on uncertain ground and possibly getting herself — and her new friend — into trouble.

"He was sort of tall, dark . . . Had gray eyes, or maybe they was blue."

Kendall nodded slowly. "You said he bought a new hat and shirt — what kind was he wearing when he came in?"

"Didn't have no hat. Shirt was a gray one — had some stains on one shoulder . . . Blood, maybe."

"It's him — sure'n hell!" George said suddenly. "Was the kind of shirt he was wearing . . . Dammit, I knew all the time he was alive! Had to be him that turned them steers back during the stampede. Weren't none of our bunch over there."

Annie, features troubled, stared at George and then at Kendall. "Why? What's he done? Ain't he one of your crew?"

"He ain't done nothing except not staying dead," Kendall replied. "And he ain't one of us — that's for damn sure!"

The girl drew back. "I — I didn't aim to get him in no trouble . . . He was nice to me and —"

"You didn't," the rustler cut in, "leastwise no more'n he's plain asking for himself . . .

156

Now, we're heading to Wichita. If you're of a mind, you can string along with us."

"I don't know," she said hesitantly. "Rather find him — keep on going."

"You'll find him, all right. Expect you already have, in fact. You just can't see him. None of us can."

"I — I ain't getting what you mean."

"Like as not he's looking at us right now. You stick with us and he'll show up sooner or later."

"Yes ma'am, lady, you do that," one of the men near the fire called. "This here drive could sure use some female companionship!"

Annie Gilmore flicked the man with a glance. She shrugged. "Sure, why not? One way of getting to Wichita." She turned to Kendall. "Seems you're the boss man — who'll it be tonight?"

The rustler grinned. "Reckon you're safe for now. Boy's have all had a hard day. All they're hunting is shut-eye." Reaching down, he picked up his blanket, handed it to her. "Roll yourself up in this. Tomorrow we'll hunt up some better duds for you to wear . . . I'll see to your horse."

Dave Bradford faded quietly into the shadows behind a stand of brush a dozen strides below the picket line. Bent low, he watched Annie Gilmore pull the woolen blanket around herself and settle beside the fire.

The outlaw called Joe took up his cover, began to search about for a suitable place for himself. Others of the party who had not already gone back to sleep, relaxed. Kendall moved to the girl's horse, took the headstall in his hand and led it toward the tethered animals. George wheeled hurriedly, followed him.

"What you think?" the older man asked anxiously in a low voice.

"I'm thinking we should've done a better job back there on Texas Flat," Kendall said gruffly, halting and securing the horse to the line. "Now we've got him to worry about — along with getting to Wichita ahead of Casey and Macklin."

George spat into the grass. "What the hell can he do? By hisself, seems, and he sure ain't fool enough to jump us alone."

"No, he would've already tried that if it was what he's thinking. I figure he's got something else in mind."

"He wouldn't be aiming to claim the herd when we get to the railhead. Be his word against ours — and we got papers saying the cattle's ours . . . Nobody'd listen to him."

Kendall grunted. "Well, you can be damned sure he's got something in his poke . . . Best thing we can do is put a bullet in him first chance we get."

"He'll figure that. Won't be crazy enough to show hisself."

"Maybe. Got a hunch that gal of Buck's could be the answer. We'll keep her hanging around. Could be she'll turn out to be the sugar that draws the fly."

"Her? Hell, she don't mean nothing to him."

"Ain't saying she does, but his kind always has a soft spot for the likes of her, and he must've showed it aplenty or she wouldn't have come traipsing out here looking for him."

"Could be, but I still don't savvy —"

"No need for you to — just leave it to me. In the morning pass the word to the boys that they're to keep a sharp eye out for somebody riding the hills. He'll likely just follow along, waiting for a chance to do whatever it is he's figuring on . . . Let's get some sleep. Aim to cover more miles tomorrow than we did today."

19

Bradford waited until the camp had quieted and then he returned to his horse and rode back to the grove.

The appearance of Annie Gilmore was a bad break. The outlaws were now certain that he was not only alive but close by and with some sort of scheme that threatened their own hopes for riches. They would be on the alert for him, searching for an opportunity to put a bullet into him and rid themselves of him for good.

He supposed he should forget staying with his herd, simply ride on to Wichita and wait for the outlaws there. Keeping under cover was bound to become more difficult as the land flattened out steadily to more barren plains and his chances to remain hidden grew smaller with each passing day.

But he was reluctant to do so. It was still a long way to the railhead and much could happen — another stampede, raids by other rustlers, thievery at the hands of Indians and homesteaders. By his presence he had been able to prevent the loss of a hundred beeves on the drive; he might be called upon to do it again . . . He'd best stay with the drive, take the risks of being seen. One fortunate thing about it, he was now aware that they were watching for him and could thus be more wary.

It had been a good plan he was following, one that was working well. He reckoned now that he'd been a fool to help Annie Gilmore, but it hadn't occurred to him that it would all end with her showing up in the rustlers' camp and tipping them off, unwittingly, to his being near. He couldn't blame her but he'd not soon forget that it was possible for a good turn to kick back the wrong way.

He shook his head, ridding himself of such a thought. There was no percentage in moaning about it now; he would simply double his caution.

The next day passed much as the one preceding with Kendall and his outlaw crew driving the cattle hard and covering far more miles than a herd ordinarily traveled. Dave skulked the brush and thinning groves at a distance and could tell little of what went on, but he did catch sight of

Annie riding along with the men and doing her bit to help.

He gave up making nightly visits into the camp, certain that Kendall would be posting a guard, so without the information usually obtained during such forays, he was in the dark if there were any changes in plans. Likely there'd been no second thoughts on the matter; they were making good time moving the cattle and at the present rate would be in Wichita days before Kurt Casey and Guy Macklin could be expected to arrive.

Conscious of that and its meaning — that they would soon have thousands of dollars to be passed between them, Kendall and George would be thinking of little else.

Time wore on, the days moving by in a weary succession of sameness as the herd progressed steadily across the wide flats. Kendall and two of the rustlers rode off once, returned with a dozen fresh horses — either bargained for or stolen from some rancher, he could not know which. The pace of the drive picked up again with the relieving of their own near exhausted mounts.

Another heavy rain struck, this time at night, but although lightning crackled across the black sky and thunder rolled and pounded, no stampede resulted. Such was due likely to the worn condition of the steers.

It became more difficult for Bradford to remain near the herd and grew to be a matter of riding either behind or ahead at a far distance with opportunities of getting a close look coming at sparse intervals.

No more time was wasted by the rustlers in the towns near which they passed as the need to reach Wichita well ahead of schedule became increasingly more important. How Kendall and his partner, George, were able to explain the haste to the remaining outlaws was a mystery to Dave but they evidently satisfied them in some way.

Supplies were picked up without interrupting the march, by the outlaw leader and Annie, who, now clad in men's clothing, had assumed that chore of cooking along with the other duties that undoubtedly fell her lot.

On the evening of the twelfth of the month, they reached the railhead and bedded the herd down along its outskirts. Dave, arriving in the settlement near midmorning, stabled his horse and checked himself into a hotel from which he could overlook the stock pens. After cleaning up, he treated himself to a meal in one of the restaurants and then settled back to wait.

Relief was running strong through him. The herd was finally at Wichita and losses had been kept to a minimum — the seven that had been killed in the first stampede plus an additional four or five that had strayed along the way being the sum total. He guessed he could ask for little better except that, in the end, he could not forget that Milt Fresno and Claude Jackson and Earl Ruskin had all died in the process of accomplishing it.

Remembering his lost crew brought a grimness to Dave Bradford's eyes, but there was a feeling of satisfaction glowing within him, too. Kendall and his outlaw partners were soon to be called to account for what they had done. His one regret was that Macklin and Casey, who had been the instigators of it all, would not be present to also pay the price he intended to exact.

That evening, with the lights of Wichita burning brightly in the overcrowded saloons and gambling halls, the streets teeming with people, Bradford strode slowly along one of the less frequented walks at the edge of the settlement. He felt the need to be careful, keep out of sight, but he did have an urge to have a final look at his cattle before turning in for the night. That next morning he could expect the rustlers to drive the herd into the pens and begin negotiations with interested buyers. Once that was completed, his time to step in would be at hand.

The cattle were quiet, tired after the final day of hard traveling. Four men were on night watch, one to a side, their fires small, flickering tongues in the darkness. Kendall and George were taking no chances on losing any more steers now that the destination had been reached.

Dave tarried awhile in the shadows of the buildings at the end of the street, smoking a cigar he had purchased at the restaurant where he had taken supper, and then, also tired and looking forward to a night of comfort in a good bed, he wheeled and headed back for the hotel.

Halfway, as he moved along the fronts of several darkened, deserted buildings, a sound close by sent a warning racing through him, brought him up short. He spun on a heel, anticipating a robbery as his hand dropped swiftly to the pistol at his hip. He had a quick glimpse of Kendall's grinning face in the feeble light, heard a second noise — one of a door opening. He started to spin again. In the next instant something crashed into the back of his head. He felt himself going down as blackness surged over him.

20

It was still night for he lay in utter darkness. Breathing was difficult, and he realized a gag had been pulled tight across his mouth. His wrists were bound together as were his ankles, and a familiar pain throbbed in his head.

He remained quiet, not certain if he was alone. And then, after several minutes during which he heard no close by sounds, he stirred, cautiously drew himself to a sitting position. The blackness of his surroundings made it near impossible to tell exactly where he was; in an empty store building, he thought, one with boarded-up windows.

Dave Bradford swore deeply. He had played right into the outlaws' hands. Failing to encounter him on the trail, they had figured he would be in Wichita awaiting them and had acted accordingly.

A search for him had been initiated. He had been spotted. Watching their chances, which had come when he went to the edge of town for a look at his herd, they had simply waited in ambush along the darkened street, knocked him out and thrown him, bound and gagged into an abandoned building. The one good thing about it was that they had not put a bullet in his head — probably for the sole reason that a gunshot echoing along the street would have drawn attention.

They might as well, he thought bitterly, struggling against his bonds. He'd likely lie there and die of thirst and starvation before anyone chanced to look inside the vacant structure.

That could be the answer — try to draw the attention of someone in the street. It was a little used section of the town he knew, but he had noticed three or four other persons on the board sidewalk while taking his stroll; perhaps there was still someone about despite the late hour . . . If he could work himself to the door — which was in the wall beyond which appeared to be a sagging, partly fallen partition dividing the room — he could thump on it with his feet.

Leaning forward, he started to throw himself full length and roll. His body checked abruptly as a band cut deep into his middle. Dave cursed vividly. Kendall and George had anticipated such an attempt; a short length of rope encircled him, tied him to a stud in the partition. He was tethered like a dog to a post.

Sweating, breathing hard, he turned his attention to the cord that locked his wrists together. The rustlers had used a piece of cotton rope, probably torn from the sash weight of one of the windows. Because of its flexibility, they had been able to link his wrists more tightly and with a closer knot.

He worked at the cord diligently, twisting his hands back and forth, placing the palms against each other and prying desperately in an effort to create slack. There was no give and after a time he abandoned the effort and settled back against the crumbling partition, tried to think of another solution.

There had to be a way out. The rustlers would complete a deal for the herd in the morning, which couldn't be many hours off. He must be there to collect or he and the other ranchers of the Cebolla Basin would come out losers — and JJ Farman and the outlaws who had taken the cattle from him would win.

Savagely impatient, he fell to working at the rope that bound his wrists again, twisting, pulling, prying. It resisted all his efforts stubbornly. He sank back once more, sucking hard for wind, sweat pouring off his body. The only answer was to cut the cotton fibers somehow, and there was nothing available with which to do that.

Likely, on the floor somewhere, he would find pieces of glass from the broken windows, but getting to them would be out of the question. The rope encircling his waist and anchoring him to the partition prevented such.

The partition . . . He frowned, strained to see the raw edges of the upright studs and their cross-braces. If he could locate a protruding nail — the head, or even the point — he might have something with which to work. Hitching his way closer to the divider, he hunched forward, eyes endeavoring to pierce the darkness that filled the room and find an extending bit of metal.

A point. He found it in one of the braces — a place where the nail had been driven in at an angle and split away. A glimmer of hope passed through him. The head of a nail would have been more effective; he could have hooked the cotton rope against it, tugged at the knot until it loosened; but the point was better than nothing at all.

Selecting a spot in the cord where it

passed over the side of his left wrist and was thus easier to work with, he began to pick at the point of the nail by placing the rope upon it and sawing his hands back and forth. At first the maneuver seemed to have little effect, and then a strand separated. He pushed it to the base of the extending nail, jerked hard. The fiber snapped.

Encouraged by that, he set himself to parting and breaking another strand. It came more readily than the first. Crowding up as near to the nail as the tether rope would allow, Dave began to work at destroying the cord feverishly, sweating freely, breathing hard, his head pounding with pain while his muscles ached from the stress he was placing upon them.

It was a slow, frustrating process. Minutes faded into hours. He felt as if his arms, raised as they were to bring the rope in contact with the nail point, were going to drop from his body. Both shoulders had gone completely numb and his back muscles pained worse than in the days when he had spent time breaking wild mustangs.

Suddenly the last strand parted. Bradford's arms sank to the floor and for a long minute he hung motionless breathing rapidly. He reached up then, tore the gag from his mouth, leaned back against the partition and gulped in great mouthfuls of free, if stale, air while the throbbing in his muscles gradually abated.

He looked up. Light was showing faintly now through the cracks around the windows. It was near dawn. He must be up and going, get himself set for the accounting he had planned . . . Kendall and George were due for a big surprise; he wasn't out of the picture yet.

In the dull grayness he glanced to the holster on his leg, swore irritably. His gun was gone. It hadn't occurred to him earlier to take note, being thoroughly engrossed in freeing himself. Now he had another problem. It wasn't serious. A weapon would not be hard to find, it was only that more delay would ensue.

Turning to the rope about his middle, he worked the knot around to the front, tore at the curled strands until they came loose and fell away. He put his attention to the cord that lashed his ankles. Heavier rope had been used — a piece of the same that was employed in tieing him to the studding, he guessed. The knots had been set tight. It would take —

He came to quick attention as a rattling at the door reached him. Someone was

172

coming to check on him, see that he had not somehow slipped his bonds during the night . . . He should have expected Kendall to take such precautions.

Forgetting the rope about his ankles, he pulled himself upright. A splintered length of the studding lay at the end of the partition. He snatched it up quickly, drew in behind the sagging wall. The door rattled again, metal clinked faintly. It had been padlocked evidently and whoever it was coming to look in on him was releasing the clasp.

A voice muttered something, was answered immediately. There were more than one — at least two in the party — and there could be more; all eight in fact. Grim, jaw set, Bradford crowded against the partition and waited.

The door swung in with a creak and someone said: "Let's hurry it up, get down to them pens. Ain't saying I don't trust Kendall, but I'd as soon be on hand when the deal's made."

"Me, too," came the reply. "Got me a funny feeling that something's going on — all that big rush to get here and such."

The first man paused somewhere in the adjoining room. "Could be but I don't see Kendall trying to put anything over on

Kurt and Macklin. They'd sure be bucking for the graveyard . . . That Macklin'd shoot a man just for looking at him slanch-ways."

"Kurt ain't no different. He —"

The first of the pair rounded the end of the partition, halted. In that same instant Dave swung the length of two-by-four. It caught the rustler across the face, crushing the yell that formed on his lips, drove him back into his partner a step behind him.

Instantly Bradford lunged forward, threw himself upon the man, slammed him back to the floor just as he recovered and sought to regain his feet. Clubbing his hands, Dave hammered his fists into the outlaw's jaw. The man groaned, lay still.

Twisting about, he glanced at the other. A dark welt had appeared across his face and blood was trickling from his broken nose and smashed lips . . . He would be a long time coming around.

Breathing heavily, sweat plastering him, Dave plucked the sheath knife the man beneath him wore on his belt and slashed the rope that bound his ankles. Rising, he then dragged both outlaws back into the inner room, and with the ropes that had been used on him, tied the pair together and gagged them with their own bandannas.

Pulling their pistols, he examined each, tested their respective feel, and choosing the one that seemed the most comfortable in his hand, jammed it into his own holster. The other weapon he tossed into a hole in the floor.

Picking up his hat he moved toward the door in long strides. He need not worry about a gun now, and that would save him time — but he was already late and should get to the loading pens as quickly as possible. Kendall and the other rustlers would be there.

He drew back the door, halted abruptly while his hand swept down for the pistol on his hip. He paused. It was Annie Gilmore. She had apparently been with the two outlaws, was waiting for them to return.

"You!" she cried, surprise jolting the word from her lips.

Bradford's hand shot out, wrapped about her wrist and drew her into the building.

"What's it to be?" he demanded harshly. "You want to be added to that pile over there in the corner — or do you want to be on your way with your mouth shut tight?"

She had recovered from the shock of meeting him so abruptly. She glanced at the two rustlers, still unconscious, shrugged. "They don't mean nothing to me. Plenty glad to get away from them . . . I've had them pawing me for damn near a month — and that's more'n enough. If it's all the same, I'll head back into town."

Bradford studied her narrowly. "Not sure I can trust you."

"You can," she said simply. "I don't owe them nothing — none of them, and you done me a favor. I ain't paying you back by telling any of them you got loose . . . They're all down there with the cattle, anyways."

"Keeping your lip buttoned is all I'm asking for," Dave said. "You got a place to go where you can keep out of sight until this is all over?"

Annie shook her head. "Nope. They — Joe and Amos, them two there, was going to set me up in a house when they got their share of the selling, pay the first month's rent for me so's I could get started. Now —"

Bradford reached into his pocket. "Here's the key to my room — number 3 at the Trail's End Hotel. Go there. I'll come later and we'll see about getting that house for you."

She took the key from him, smiled. "I'm

obliged to you again, Mister Bradford," she said, and turned to the door. "Good luck."

He bobbed his head at her and stepped out onto the walk. It would take more than luck to get him through the next few hours, alive.

21

That Kendall and George were in a hurry to complete a sale of the herd was apparent, for when Dave Bradford reached the end of the street that led on to the pens, the cattle had been brought in and were being tallied.

Circling wide, Dave came in behind one of the lower corrals, and moving along its board sides, moved in close to where he could see and hear all that was taking place while still remaining unnoticed.

The two rustlers, standing on either side of a man wearing a business suit over which he had drawn a tan-colored duster, were intently watching the steers as they crowded into a narrow chute which led into a pen. The remainder of the rustlers, mounted, and with short ropes in their hand, were keeping the stock pressing into the passageway. A steadily thickening pall hung over the entire area.

Onlookers began to gather, businessmen from the town now awake to the new day, loafers who spent their time between the saloons, the cattle yards and the stables; stray cowhands looking for work, a few gaudily dressed women lined up and waiting for the riders primed to celebrate as soon as they were paid off.

The last of the steers lunged into the chute, rushed to overtake the others already milling about in the pen. The man in the duster made a final mark on his tally sheet, did some hurried figuring and then turned to Kendall.

"I make it five hundred and forty-eight head, Mr. Kendall . . . At fourteen dollars per, the total comes out to seven thousand six hundred and seventy-two dollars."

Kendall glanced at George, swallowed hard, and grinned. "Fair enough."

Dave frowned. The market had evidently slipped a bit. He had expected to get fifteen, possibly sixteen dollars each for his stock! He grinned wryly. Considering all that had happened since that day at noon when he had moved the herd out from the Cebolla Basin, he reckoned he should be grateful he would be getting anything at all.

"Here's your draft," the buyer said, handing an oblong slip of paper to Kendall. "Just take it over to the bank and they'll —"

"I'll do the taking . . ."

Dave Bradford's attention pivoted to the crowd that had gathered in front of the pen. Surprise rocked him as Kurt Casey, followed by Guy Macklin and the rustler called Deke, pushed into the open.

Understanding swept through him a moment later. Deke, left for dead, and determined to get even with the two who had double-crossed him, had hurried back to the J-Bar-J, warned Casey and Macklin of the plan to cheat them. The two gunmen had reacted at once with a countering scheme of their own and ridden in early to be on hand. Dave smiled bleakly. Matters were going to work out his way after all.

The cattle buyer was staring blankly at Kurt. He shook his head. "I don't understand — I thought Mr. Kendall was the owner."

Macklin, arms hanging loosely at his sides, considered Kendall humorlessly. "Speak up, Mr. Kendall," he said in his dry, sardonic way. "Why don't you tell him who them steers belong to?"

"Sure, you do that," Casey added, and took a step to one side, permitting himself to line up with Macklin, facing the two rustlers. The rest of the outlaw crew, still on their horses, looked on, not understanding all that was taking place before them.

Kendall cast a hurried glance at George, forced a smile to his lips. "Why, you do, Kurt . . . You and Macklin. We all know that."

"Just happened we got here a couple of days earlier'n we figured," George, at last finding his voice, added hastily. "We was only going ahead and making the deal for you."

Casey spat into the dust. "Well, now, that's mighty nice of you boys, only it ain't the way Deke tells it."

The cattle buyer rubbed at his jaw nervously, started to thrust the draft back into his pocket. "Now, maybe — if there's some dispute about the ownership — I —"

"No dispute," Kurt cut in quietly. "You got the papers on them steers, didn't you?"

"Well, yes —"

"And they was all right, wasn't they?"

"Yes. The brands all tallied out —"

"Then you ain't got no call to squawk or start backing down. I'll just take that draft, and me and my partner here'll settle with Mr. Kendall and the others. That suit you?"

The buyer hesitated briefly, and then handed the draft to Casey. "Of course. Just want everything to be all legal and in order."

"That's what it is," Kurt Casey said, the same frozen smile still on his lips. "All legal and such. I'm obliged to you."

"Oh, no, I'm obliged to you, Mister — Mister —"

"Casey."

"Casey . . . Be happy to deal with you again someday. Fine bunch of beef you sent in — a little on the light side maybe from the drive, but prime stock just the same. Hope I can deal with you again next year."

"Maybe you will," Kurt said, tucking the draft into a shirt pocket. He glanced to the men still on their horses. "Be cashing this order right away. You want your pay, meet me at the Gold Dollar Saloon — down on Douglas Street — in one hour."

Ignoring the faint cheer that went up, Casey shifted his hooded eyes to Kendall and George. "Goes for you, too . . . You feel like you want to collect, meet us there."

Kendall bobbed his head nervously. "Sure, Kurt . . . sure."

Casey wheeled lazily. Macklin, his gaze lingering on the two men for another few seconds, turned also, and with Deke tagging their heels, both headed back into town.

At once Dave Bradford cut back between the loading pens, and crossing to an alley that ran parallel to the street, kept pace with the three men to the intersection where the Cattleman's Trust Bank stood.

Halting there, he watched them enter the building. Then, drawing his pistol and checking its loads, he moved in behind a surrey that had been drawn up to the hitchrack fronting the establishment. With it between him and the glass-door entrance to the place, forming an effective screen, he waited.

He should have gone to the town marshal, he knew, but there hadn't been time. Too, it was a matter better first handled and then explained. If all went well there'd be no need for the law coming into the picture, anyway, except to make the necessary arrests for murder, rustling and horse stealing. But if Casey and Macklin elected to make a stand and fight — which he secretly hoped they would do — then he would have some explaining to —

Dave Bradford drew up slowly. The three men were emerging from the bank. Casey had a thick sheaf of currency in his hand, and a wide smile split his mouth.

Guy Macklin was a softly walking shadow to his left while a stride behind them came the rustler named Deke.

"Now, I reckon we —"

At Casey's words Bradford stepped from the shadow of the surrey.

"I'll take my money," he said in a cold, level voice.

The men pulled up short. Astonishment blanked Kurt Casey's face. Macklin's expression did not change. He reacted in the same breath, hand blurring, sweeping upward, metal glinting in the strong sunlight.

Dave sidestepped, buckled forward, drew. His weapon blasted. Macklin, gun only half up, staggered as a bullet slammed into him. Without moving Bradford triggered a second shot, firing in the same breath of time that Casey brought his pistol into play. The two reports blended as one. Dave felt the lead slug whip at the slack in his sleeve, saw Kurt lurch, go to his knees, scattering the bills before him as he fell.

Crouched, gun still poised, Bradford fixed his burning stare on Deke. "You?" he murmured.

The outlaw raised his hands hastily. Voices were yelling in the street and boots were pounding on the sun baked ground.

"No — I give up! Don't shoot!" Deke answered in high-pitched tones.

Dave straightened slowly, the hard, brittle tension that had gripped him, beginning to fade. He bucked his head at the rustler.

"Pick up that money — hand it to me."

Deke crossed hurriedly to where Kurt Casey lay, knelt down and collected the scattered bills. Shaping them into a pack, he placed them in Bradford's palm.

In that same moment a low, harsh voice at Dave's shoulder said: "I've got a gun on you, mister. Drop yours."

Bradford allowed his weapon to fall to the ground. He pivoted slowly, faced a bearded man wearing a deputy marshal's star.

"They're rustlers," he said. "Killers, too. They raided my herd, shot three of my crew and left me for dead . . . Then drove my cattle here and sold them. I was just taking my money."

The lawman studied him dispassionately. "You got proof of that?"

Dave jerked a thumb at Deke. "He's one of them. You'll find some more at the loading pens or maybe at the Gold Dollar Saloon. I left a couple tied up in an old building down the street a ways . . .

Reckon at least one of them will talk."

The deputy's wooden expression did not change. Dave shrugged, said: "You need more proof take a close look at the cattle they sold off. They'll all have blotted brands. Or, if you want, get in touch with the ranchers where I came from — the Cebolla Basin. Part of the herd belonged to them."

"He'll be telling you the truth, Charley," a voice spoke up from the crowd. "I know this fellow — name's Dave Bradford. Worked under me back in Omaha for a spell."

Dave shifted his gaze to the speaker, an elderly man with shoulder length, iron gray hair, pushing his way through the by-standers . . . Tom Gordon. He had been the marshal in Omaha, was apparently now serving in the same capacity in Wichita.

"Know them dead ones, too. You'll find wanted dodgers for them back in my office."

Dave bent over, retrieved his pistol, deliberately punched out the empties and thumbed fresh loads into the cylinder. Holstering the weapon, he faced Gordon and extended his hand.

"Obliged, Tom . . . Good to see you again."

The old lawman took Bradford's fingers

into his own, pressed, nodded coolly. "You know better'n to walk into a man's town, shoot it out with somebody —"

"No time," Dave cut in quietly. "They didn't give me a choice." He swung his eyes then to Deke. "Farman in on this thing all the way?"

He was certain of the fact but he wanted to hear it from the rustlers before he headed back to the Basin to confront the rancher.

Deke, hands lifted as the deputy moved in behind him, nodded. "Sure was — all the way. We was told to do what we had to do in keeping you from crossing Texas Flat."

"Even if it meant killing?"

Deke looked down. "Even killing."

The corners of Dave Bradford's jaw hardened, showed white through the sun and wind burn of his skin. It was far from over yet . . . He shifted his attention back to Gordon.

"You know where to find me, Tom, if you need me . . . So long."

22

Twelve days later Dave Bradford rode onto the hardpack fronting JJ Farman's ranch-house. He was gray with dust, sweat stained, and weariness was a heavy burden riding his shoulders. But there was no diminution of the purpose that burned within him.

It was near midday. He pulled the black, which had leaned out into a pretty fair trail horse, to a halt directly in front of the house.

"Farman!" he shouted.

A chair scraped against the floor inside. A moment later the screen door flung back and the rancher stood framed in the opening. Vague motion at the corner of the building caught Dave's eye, and glancing to that point, he saw two J-Bar-J punchers easing into view. He dropped a hand to the pistol on his hip. They froze instantly.

Farman was staring at him, disbelief filling his features. He recovered, folded his arms across his chest and moved to the edge of the porch.

"What the hell do you want?" he demanded.

"Letting you know something. The deal you cooked up to keep me from crossing Texas Flat didn't work. Herd's been sold and I've got the cash here in my pocket."

"So?"

"Your gunhawks are laying in Boot Hill in Wichita — both of them. Rest of the bunch you sent to stop me are in jail there — waiting to be tried for murder, rustling, and horse stealing."

JJ Farman's expression did not change.

"Three of my men are dead," Bradford continued. "Casey and Macklin squares me for two of them. You're elected to be number three — if I ever catch you on Texas Flat again. That clear?"

The rancher's face was now turning red slowly. "You can't keep me off! It's open range."

"Not what you told me and my friends. It's open, and it's going to stay open to everybody but you and J-Bar-J cattle. You tried keeping us off — I'm turning it around and keeping you off — from here on."

Abruptly Bradford wheeled the black around, and with a warning glance at the two punchers still lounging against the corner of the house, rode from the yard.

It was a long, tense minute, moving off, his back to the rancher and his hired hands. Farman had been wearing no gun but both punchers were armed, and he sat his saddle in rigid anticipation, ready to whirl at the first intuitive impulse, pistol firing. But he gained the end of the cleared ground and cut in behind the tamarisk windbreak without incident.

He breathed deeper. It had, perhaps, been a damned fool thing to do, but he felt it necessary. Farman had to be told that he'd failed, and made to realize he was not feared. It was the only way to keep Texas Flat open for all to use.

Unless — Dave paused on the crest of a hill south of Farman's and looked back . . . The rancher was a proud man who did not know how to accept defeat. He could make a final, desperate attempt to salvage that pride and preserve his autocratic stature . . . It would be like him.

There were no signs of pursuit. Dave shrugged. He was taking no assurance from that, however, was listening instead to a small inner voice pushing at him urgently, setting up a warning, and putting him on guard. He'd watch, take care — just in the event that Farman ran true to form with all those of his kind, and refused to admit he had lost.

Brushing sweat from his face, Dave rode on, soon moving past the marker that indicated J-Bar-J range and the entrance to the upper portion of Texas Flat. The country was some rougher here, broken by small arroyos and low, scattered buttes and overgrown by snakeweed and rabbitbrush.

He wasn't too far from the Cebolla Basin and home, he thought, and sighed gratefully. It would be good to get back, to bring word of the success despite all that had happened, to parcel out the money due that was so important to the others . . . And it would be wonderful to hold Sirral again in his arms . . . They could go ahead now with their plans for the future, for the home and ranch he'd always dreamed and worked for.

The one dark note was that he returned alone; three fine men lay dead under the soil of Texas Flat as a result of Farman's greed and he could not, and would not, forget that. Nor would he ever let the others forget it. Their deaths must serve as a monument, as a warning to all that there would be other JJ Farmans to come —

The dry, flat crack of a rifle echoed hollowly through the hot air. In that same instant the black stumbled, plunged forward. Dave, clawing at the pistol on his hip, kicked free of the stirrups, and threw himself clear of the thrashing horse. He struck the ground full length, rolled frantically for a clump of sage a stride away.

The rifle barked again. White hot pain seared through him as a bullet smashed into his left arm. He jerked aside, tried to see, to locate the bushwacker. Two more guns opened up, coming from the opposite quarters. They had him pocketed neatly . . . Three of them. Likely Farman and the two he'd seen standing at the corner of the house.

A rider rode suddenly into view on his right. One of the pair. He was half-standing in his stirrups, neck craned, as he looked about. Evidently he had lost sight of his intended target. Bradford rolled to his back, ignoring pain, and brought up his weapon just as the puncher located him.

He pressed off a shot, saw the man fall heavily. Instantly the second rider drove in from the left, coming up fast. Dave threw himself half around, edged up close to the bank of the gully in which he lay.

The thud of the horse's hoofs grew louder, ceased abruptly. The man was directly above him. Dave leaned back, snapped a shot at the overhanging shadow. The puncher yelled, toppled from his saddle as the frightened horse shied away.

Through the haze of acrid smoke drifting down the wash, Bradford saw the vague figure of the third man — Farman. The rancher had dropped from his mount and worked in close. He stood at the end of the gully, pistol raised — leveled.

Dave heaved himself to one side, fired blindly as the rancher got off his shot. Sand spurted in Bradford's face as he rolled fast, pressed off a second bullet, reversed himself to twist away again.

No challenging gunshot came. Bradford, now hard against the wall of the wash, fixed his eyes on the rancher. Farman was leaning forward, face contorted, shoulders hunched. The pistol in his hand had tipped down, smoke trickling from its muzzle. Suddenly the rancher's legs gave way and he tumbled limply into the gully.

Breathing hard, pain coursing through his body, Bradford lay quiet for a long minute. Finally, he drew himself upright. Holding the pistol in his numbed left hand, he rodded out the spent cartridges, and reloading, dropped it into its holster. Other J-Bar-J men, hearing the gunshots, might appear . . . He would be ready for them.

Without a second glance at Farman, he climbed from the gully and walked stiffly to where his horse lay. The black was dead — had probably been dead the moment he went down. Dave stared at the gelding for a time, stirred by pity. The black had been a good mount.

Arm hanging rigidly at his side, he leaned over, pulled free his saddlebags and turned toward the rancher's horse, standing a few yards below the wash . . . He'd send someone over to pick up his gear . . . And he'd get word to the J-Bar-J, too, have them see to the bodies of the three men.

Reaching the horse, Dave pulled himself wearily onto the saddle, and wheeling about, pointed for the Basin . . . It was all over with now.

We hope you have enjoyed this Large Print book. Other Thorndike, Wheeler or Chivers Press Large Print books are available at your library or directly from the publishers.

For more information about current and upcoming titles, please call or write, without obligation, to:

Publisher
Thorndike Press
295 Kennedy Memorial Drive
Waterville, ME   04901
Tel. (800) 223-1244

Or visit our Web site at:
www.gale.com/thorndike
www.gale.com/wheeler

OR

Chivers Large Print
published by BBC Audiobooks Ltd
St James House, The Square
Lower Bristol Road
Bath BA2 3SB
England
Tel. +44(0) 800 136919
email: bbcaudiobooks@bbc.co.uk
www.bbcaudiobooks.co.uk

All our Large Print titles are designed for easy reading, and all our books are made to